Dwa
3/9/08

Run for Your Life

"Do it *now!*"

And Tom did whirl, duck, and run. Dan swore and raised his pistol to shoot Tom in the back. But Longarm slammed his shoulder into the Irishman, then spun around and kicked out desperately, trying to knock the other two men down.

Shots exploded and Longarm's hand streaked across his waist for his own weapon, which he drew and fired in one smooth, well-practiced motion. He shot one of the men in the belly, and then he tripped over something and fell . . . which probably saved his life . . .

D0711447

DON'T MISS THESE
ALL-ACTION WESTERN SERIES
FROM THE BERKLEY PUBLISHING GROUP

THE GUNSMITH by J. R. Roberts

Clint Adams was a legend among lawmen, outlaws, and ladies. They called him . . . the Gunsmith.

LONGARM by Tabor Evans

The popular long-running series about Deputy U.S. Marshal Custis Long—his life, his loves, his fight for justice.

SLOCUM by Jake Logan

Today's longest-running action Western. John Slocum rides a deadly trail of hot blood and cold steel.

BUSHWHACKERS by B. J. Lanagan

An action-packed series by the creators of Longarm! The rousing adventures of the most brutal gang of cutthroats ever assembled—Quantrill's Raiders.

DIAMONDBACK by Guy Brewer

Dex Yancey is Diamondback, a Southern gentleman turned con man when his brother cheats him out of the family fortune. Ladies love him. Gamblers hate him. But nobody pulls one over on Dex . . .

WILDGUN by Jack Hanson

The blazing adventures of mountain man Will Barlow—from the creators of Longarm!

TEXAS TRACKER by Tom Calhoun

J.T. Law: the most relentless—and dangerous—manhunter in all Texas. Where sheriffs and posses fail, he's the best man to bring in the most vicious outlaws—for a price.

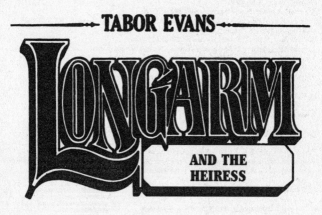

TABOR EVANS

LONGARM

AND THE HEIRESS

JOVE BOOKS, NEW YORK

THE BERKLEY PUBLISHING GROUP
Published by the Penguin Group
Penguin Group (USA) Inc.
375 Hudson Street, New York, New York 10014, USA
Penguin Group (Canada), 90 Eglinton Avenue East, Suite 700, Toronto, Ontario M4P 2Y3, Canada
(a division of Pearson Penguin Canada Inc.)
Penguin Books Ltd., 80 Strand, London WC2R 0RL, England
Penguin Group Ireland, 25 St. Stephen's Green, Dublin 2, Ireland (a division of Penguin Books Ltd.)
Penguin Group (Australia), 250 Camberwell Road, Camberwell, Victoria 3124, Australia
(a division of Pearson Australia Group Pty. Ltd.)
Penguin Books India Pvt. Ltd., 11 Community Centre, Panchsheel Park, New Delhi—110 017, India
Penguin Group (NZ), 67 Apollo Drive, Rosedale, North Shore 0632, New Zealand
(a division of Pearson New Zealand Ltd.)
Penguin Books (South Africa) (Pty.) Ltd., 24 Sturdee Avenue, Rosebank, Johannesburg 2196,
South Africa

Penguin Books Ltd., Registered Offices: 80 Strand, London WC2R 0RL, England

This is a work of fiction. Names, characters, places, and incidents either are the product of the author's imagination or are used fictitiously, and any resemblance to actual persons, living or dead, business establishments, events, or locales is entirely coincidental.

LONGARM AND THE HEIRESS

A Jove Book / published by arrangement with the author

PRINTING HISTORY
Jove edition / February 2008

Copyright © 2008 by The Berkley Publishing Group.
Cover illustration by Miro Sinovcic.

All rights reserved.
No part of this book may be reproduced, scanned, or distributed in any printed or electronic form without permission. Please do not participate in or encourage piracy of copyrighted materials in violation of the author's rights. Purchase only authorized editions.
For information, address: The Berkley Publishing Group,
a division of Penguin Group (USA) Inc.,
375 Hudson Street, New York, New York 10014.

ISBN: 978-0-515-14404-8

JOVE®
Jove Books are published by The Berkley Publishing Group,
a division of Penguin Group (USA) Inc.,
375 Hudson Street, New York, New York 10014.
JOVE is a registered trademark of Penguin Group (USA) Inc.
The "J" design is a trademark belonging to Penguin Group (USA) Inc.

PRINTED IN THE UNITED STATES OF AMERICA

10 9 8 7 6 5 4 3 2 1

If you purchased this book without a cover, you should be aware that this book is stolen property. It was reported as "unsold and destroyed" to the publisher, and neither the author nor the publisher has received any payment for this "stripped book."

Chapter 1

Deputy United States Marshal Custis Long was searching
for a stray cat that had taken up residence in his Denver
apartment on a night when it was raining hard. He had
named the cat "Tiger" because it was an orange tabby that
murdered a mouse or a rat almost daily. Tiger was big, ath-
letic, and handsome in the exact same way that most women
viewed Longarm.

"Tiger! Here, boy! Where are you, cat!"

Longarm was sopping wet and hatless. He'd been
caught in the sudden downpour in his back alley, and the
rain was sheeting off the rooftops, making him feel cold
and miserable. The back alley was dim and filthy, cluttered
mountains of uncollected trash. Longarm was thinking that,
when he caught Tiger, he was either going to drown the
animal or figure a way to keep it out of this wretched alley.
Trouble was, like most cats, Tiger was completely independent.

"Tiger!"

Suddenly Longarm heard a low moan coming from behind one of the piles of rubbish. He put his hand to his brow
and peered intently into the darkness to see Tiger sitting

atop a ripped and discarded mattress. The tomcat stared at Longarm for a long moment and then it yowled pitifully.

"What the hell are you doing out here in the rain!" Longarm ranted. "I left my window open for you to come on in and get dry. You got a warm bed and food in my apartment but you're too dumb or stubborn to come inside."

Tiger meowed and swished his tail.

"Well, come on!" Longarm said crossly. "A fella could catch his death of a cold out here in this filth and downpour."

Longarm turned to go but Tiger didn't follow. Instead, the big orange tomcat let out another yowl, one so high and sad that Longarm was stopped in his tracks. He turned back and said, "Did you lose a friend in that pile of trash? Is that it?"

Tiger hung his head and looked so miserable that Longarm could not leave the animal but instead went to see why it wouldn't tag along with him to his nearby apartment.

That's when he saw the small human hand that protruded from under the mattress. Longarm's blood suddenly went cold and he scrambled up the pile of filth and tore away the soggy mattress, sending Tiger flying.

"Oh my gawd!" he whispered, staring at the battered body of a young woman and her newborn child.

The baby was blue and obviously dead. But the young woman still had a little color in her face where it wasn't so badly beaten and swollen. Both of her eyes had been hammered by either fists or a club until they were just lumps of flesh with slits of eyelash. She was clothed, though only with a torn and flimsy cotton garment that would not have protected her from a chill breeze. The woman's feet were bare as were both of her arms.

"Can you hear me!" he said, bending down over the woman and trying not to gag from the stench in his nostrils.

As expected, the woman didn't respond. Longarm took her slender wrist and felt for a pulse. It was there, but barely.

A bolt of lightning shot across the angry sky and speared into the alleyway. It struck one of the piles of rubbish and set it ablaze despite the wetness. Longarm grabbed the woman up in his arms, turned, and raced toward the back landing of his apartment. He hated to leave the newborn child, but he'd come back for it as soon as he could. There was no hard choice in this matter; the woman yet lived and the baby was already dead.

Longarm banged on the door of the apartment managers, a sweet old couple named Harney. "Hey!" he called. "Open up!"

"Who is it!"

"Custis Long. I've got a woman here and she needs help fast!"

The Harney couple recognized Longarm's loud voice and unbolted their door. When they saw—and smelled— the limp body of the woman, they recoiled in shock.

The old man's hand flew to his face and his eyes widened with horror. "What—"

"I don't know," Longarm said, cutting off the question. "This poor young lady and her baby were buried under a ruined mattress dumped in our back alley. The baby is dead. It might have been beaten to death by the same person who tried to kill and then hide this young woman, leaving her to die. Or the baby might have been stillborn. It'll take a doctor to decide."

"What kind of a monster could have done such a horrible act!" Mrs. Harney cried, tears springing to her eyes.

"And right behind our apartment!" Mr. Harney breathed, looking as if he might faint.

Longarm could see that the old couple was too rattled and upset to be of much help so he changed his plan.

3

"First things first," Longarm said, brushing past the couple and exiting their door. "I'll take the lady upstairs and try to warm her up and keep her alive. One of you hurry outside and bring Doc Potter on the run."

"But what if the doctor is already on another emergency!" Mrs. Harney cried, wringing her hands in despair.

"Then go three doors farther down the street and summon Doc Lander. Either doctor will do. Hurry!"

Longarm's apartment was on the second floor. He'd lived there for nearly two years and liked the place. It was safe, cheap, and he always knew that Mr. and Mrs. Harney watched over it as carefully as if it were their own residence.

He had not locked his door when he'd gone looking for Tiger so he got inside easily enough and then laid the young woman down on his bed. She smelled awful and he'd need to throw out his bedding, but that wasn't even worth worrying about under these dire circumstances.

Longarm knew the first thing he had to do was to get the woman out of her sopping wet dress and then get her warm. In the good light of his bedside lamp he could see that she was blue with cold, chilled to the very bone. Her breathing was barely that of a whisper and it rattled in her throat. She might have the pneumonia and die on him any minute.

Normally, he would have waited until a woman came to undress this poor waif, but this was not a time for niceties so he simply tore off the thin cotton dress and then jumped over to his stove where he kept a pot of water warm for coffee.

Longarm doused a rag into the pot, tested the temperature on his forearm, and then went back to the unconscious woman and began to wash her with the hot water. She was in her twenties, he realized, with large breasts probably filled with milk that would now never be needed by a suckling child. Longarm guessed that she was about five and a half feet tall, but not weighing much more than a hundred pounds.

Longarm rubbed the dirty, violated flesh, noting how the woman had been beaten often and, judging from the scars, for many years. He felt a rage building inside him and a desire to find out who could have done such a terrible thing to someone so small and helpless. He'd been a law officer for enough years to know that there were men capable of vile deeds such as this, but it was always a shock to see the evidence of their unbridled savagery.

The woman took a deep, shuddering breath and then let out a terrible scream as her eyes barely managed to squeeze open. Her scream of terror was so real and intense that it knifed into Longarm's very core. She began to thrash and her screaming increased in intensity.

"Easy," Longarm soothed, trying to hold her down. "It's going to be all right. You're going to live. I won't hurt you. Not like the other man."

"My baby!" she cried. "Where is my baby!"

Longarm leaned over the naked, battered woman and saw the madness in her eyes. He wasn't sure if she would even understand what he said to her, yet he had a duty to try.

"Your baby is dead," he explained quietly. "I'm sorry, but you have to know the truth. What's your name, and who did this to you? I'm a federal officer of the law and I mean to see that they pay for this!"

"Dead? Dead!"

She struggled hard and tried desperately to strike him, but he held her wrists tightly until what little strength she possessed bled out and was gone. She convulsed and fainted.

Longarm studied her violated body and felt an overwhelming sense of anger and pity. Even a stray and vicious cur should not have been treated so badly as this person. Who was she? Who was the father of her poor dead baby?

And why on earth had anyone been as callous and cruel as to leave her to die in a pile of stinking rubbish?

"I'll make it a point to get to the bottom of this," Longarm promised the cold, still woman. "By damned, when I catch the man who left you to die, I'll make him wish *he* had died!"

Longarm finished washing the unconscious woman. It took all the hot water he had on his stove and three towels to scrub away the grime. And what was below it wasn't a pretty sight. Not with all the bruises and scars, it wasn't.

When he had washed the woman's skin as well as he could manage, Longarm washed her hair. It was dark blond and wavy. He supposed, had she not been beaten beyond recognition, the woman would have been pretty.

Finally satisfied that he'd done the best that he could, Longarm covered the woman with blankets and took a seat to wait for the doctor. He didn't have long to wait.

"What happened?" Doc Lander said, hurrying into Longarm's apartment with water cascading off his hat and coat.

"I found her in the alley," Longarm said. "And her baby, which I'll go down and recover."

Lander was in his forties and was really a tooth puller, but he'd studied some medical books and become quite proficient in his medical practice over the years. Longarm had seen him extract bullets and sew up some bad knife wounds.

"My gawd!" the doctor breathed when he pulled back the blankets. "What kind of animal would do this to another human being?"

"I mean to find out," Longarm said. "She came awake for a moment and started fighting me and screaming. Doc, I've never seen such fear in anyone's eyes as she had in hers."

"Small wonder." The doctor made a quick examination. "You cleaned her up?"

6

"As best that I could," Longarm replied.

The doctor took her pulse and peeled back her eyelids. "Concussion," he said. "She's had severe trauma to the head. She might even be blind."

"I don't think so," Longarm said. "I think she saw me plainly."

"I hope you're right about that. But someone has used a club on her head and body. Even big fists couldn't do this much physical damage."

"What can you do for her, Doc?"

"Not much. You've cleaned her up and the main thing is that she's getting warm again."

"Her lungs sound awful. You think she's got the pneumonia?"

The doctor put his ear to her chest and listened to the faint rattle. "She's got it all right. If she was older, I'd say she had no chance to live. But being so young, she has a slim, fighting chance."

"What should I do with her?"

"When this storm passes, I'll have her taken to the hospital."

Longarm frowned. "The one where they take the people with some money . . . or the other one where all the poor go?"

The doctor shrugged. "I doubt she can pay to go to Saint Joseph, so she'll have to go to the other."

Longarm started to protest, but then he shut his mouth. This girl was not his concern. She was a stranger and, most likely, a prostitute.

"I'll leave some medicine that she can take if she wakes up and you can get her to swallow it," Lander said, reaching for his bag. "And in the morning—weather permitting— I'll see that an ambulance comes for her."

"What about her dead baby?"

The doc shrugged. "Can you retrieve it and take it to the mortuary?"

"Yeah," Longarm said. "I can do that much."

"You're a damn good man, Deputy Marshal Custis Long," the doc said. "And I'm sorry this happened."

"Me, too," Longarm said. "But someone is going to pay for what they did to that young mother and her baby." Longarm's voice grew hard as an anvil. "I'll make a pledge to that, Doc. I'll get to the bottom of this and someone *is* going to pay."

"I've no doubt about that," Doc Lander said, looking into Longarm's cold eyes. "And when you catch and arrest the man, I hope he gets the hangman's noose and it chokes him slowly to death."

"Me, too," Longarm said. "When you go downstairs, would you ask Mr. and Mrs. Harney to come up here and stay with this young lady until I retrieve the baby and my cat?"

"Your cat?" The doctor's eyebrows shot up in question.

"Yeah. His name is Tiger and I've sort of developed a fondness for him even though he's just a stray."

"You've a good heart, Marshal."

"Don't ever tell that to my enemies or the men I've sent to prison, Doc. Because, if you did, they'd call you either a damned fool or a liar."

Lander managed a thin smile until he glanced back at the disfigured and discolored face of the young woman. Then his smiled vanished and he headed for the door with a grim expression.

A few minutes later, Mrs. Harney came upstairs to sit with the young woman. Longarm put his wet coat and hat back on and headed downstairs and then out into the alley. The storm hadn't let up a lick. It was a most awful night to be anywhere but indoors.

Longarm found the dead baby, which he gathered in his arms. He used one of the dirty towels he'd cleaned the mother with to wrap the little body and then, head down and spirits low, he trod off to the mortuary.

Behind him, a cold, wet, and utterly miserable Tiger huddled under a dented washbasin and wailed piteously.

Chapter 2

By the time Longarm returned to his apartment, he was soaked to the skin and shaking with cold. But he had taken the dead baby to the mortician and now his cat, Tiger, was cradled in his powerful arms.

"Next time you want to go out in a storm like this," Longarm warned the cat, "I'd appreciate it if you'd stay out of that back alley. I doubt that I could stand any more terrible surprises like the one you led me into tonight."

Tiger meowed softly and went over to the stove where he began to devour all the food that was in his dish. Afterward, he coiled up near the heat of Longarm's stove, shut his eyes, and immediately went to sleep.

Longarm went into his bedroom. Poor old Mrs. Harney was sound asleep in a chair beside the bed. The beaten young woman was also sleeping. "Mrs. Harney," Longarm said, waking the older woman, "I'm back, so you can go down to your own bed now."

Mrs. Harney nodded, rose unsteadily to her feet, and tottered to the hallway door. She looked back and said, "Custis, I didn't think it possible that someone could beat another

11

human being so savagely. Catch whoever did that and punish them . . . please?"

"With any luck, Mrs. Harney, the young woman I found last night will make a complete recovery and she'll be able to tell me who did this despicable deed. And you can rest assured that when I find that man, he will wish he had never been born."

"Good!"

Now looking even older than her advanced years, Mrs. Harney closed the door. Longarm shrugged out of his wet clothes and then toweled off. He found some warm clothes and a bottle of whiskey that would warm his insides. Slumping over his little kitchen table, Longarm tossed down three stiff shots of whiskey and finally felt the icy coldness in him began to thaw. In the other room, the unnamed girl slept fitfully, occasionally waking up with a cry and a confused start. But Tiger, who had started this whole evening on the downslide, slept peacefully with neither guilt nor regret.

In the morning it was still raining with no sign of letup. Longarm would normally have gone to his job at the federal office building, but he could not leave the young woman, so he made a pot of strong coffee and found an unread newspaper.

At about ten o'clock, the girl awoke with a cry, causing Longarm to hurry into his bedroom. "Don't be afraid," he said, standing back in case she thought him threatening. "You're going to be all right."

"Who are *you*!"

"My name is Custis Long. I'm a deputy marshal and I found you last night out in the storm."

She glanced around wildly. "My baby! Where's my baby!"

Longarm took a deep breath, then blurted, "He's dead, miss. I'm very sorry. I've taken him to a fine mortuary where they will see that he is . . ." Longarm didn't know what more to say so he clamped his mouth shut.

The woman began to sob. She covered her poor face with both hands and wept bitter tears. Longarm had never been able to watch a woman weep, so he went back into the kitchen and sat down to drink more coffee and just stare through the window at the falling rain. Tiger leaped up and settled into his lap. Longarm petted the cat and said, "Look at all the damn rain we're getting. I'll bet the poor people living outdoors near Cherry Creek are probably either washed away or taking shelter on higher ground."

Tiger purred contentedly and a few minutes later, the girl staggered out of the bedroom with the blanket wrapped around her and sat down at the table with Longarm. Her hair was tangled and she looked like death warmed over.

"Coffee?" Longarm offered. "But I have to warn you that I make it mighty strong."

She managed to nod her head, wincing with pain. "I feel dizzy and kind of sick. My head throbs and aches. Maybe the coffee will clear my brain."

"A doctor saw you last night and said you have a concussion."

"What does that mean?"

"It means that someone hit you on the head so hard that it bruised your brain. Maybe caused some bleeding inside your skull. I think that you're lucky to be alive."

"I don't feel either lucky or alive," she whispered as Longarm poured her a cup of steaming coffee. "Who did this to me and my poor baby?"

She started to cry again so Longarm waited until she regained her composure before he said, "I was hoping you could tell me who did it so that I could arrest him. Given that your baby is dead, he would be tried for murder and most likely hanged. That would no doubt give us both a good deal of satisfaction, miss."

She slowly shook her aching head. "I don't remember much of what happened last night. It's all . . . all a blur."

"Drink your coffee. If Doc Lander saw you sitting up this morning at my table, he'd give me hell. You should be resting in bed."

The young woman didn't seem to be listening. She sipped the coffee and managed a faint smile of gratitude. "Tastes good."

Longarm had feared that she would find it much too strong, but she didn't seem to mind.

Through her black and swollen eyes she regarded Tiger. "I love cats," she said absently. "Can I pet him?"

"You know how independent cats are," Longarm said, going over to retrieve Tiger and handing him to the young woman. "You can give it a try, but he might not like it."

But to Longarm's surprise, Tiger did seem to like being petted by the stranger. "He's nice," she said. "But he smells bad and needs to be washed and brushed."

"Yeah, I suppose so." Longarm didn't think Tiger would go for being washed or brushed. "Don't you remember what happened last night? What's your name, and where do you live?"

She was looking down at Tiger and now she raised her head and sniffled. "I . . . I don't know," she said, suddenly letting loose of Tiger and cradling her head in her hands. "When I try to think, my head hurts even worse. It's so bad that I want to scream."

"You did a lot of that last night," Longarm told her. "You had some bad nightmares. Miss, I don't mean to be personal, but you carry a lot of old scars. I think that you've been treated real badly for a long, long time. And that makes it all the more important for me to find out who did this to you and your baby."

She began to cry again and Longarm knew that he was pressing too hard. "I'll help you back to bed," he said, feeling guilty. "Later, you'll be taken to a hospital and—"

"No!"

Longarm started. "Miss, I said a *hospital*. Did you hear me or miss my meaning?"

"No hospital!" The woman began to shake uncontrollably.

Longarm helped her back into his bed. "Take it easy," he said quietly. "There's no need to get upset. Just . . . Just lie still. Try to go back to sleep for a while."

"Where will you be?"

Longarm yawned. "It was a bad night and the day hasn't gotten a whole hell of a lot better. I was thinking of stretching out on my old couch and trying to sleep for a couple of hours."

"This is your bed. Lie down beside me," she said. "We can both sleep awhile."

Longarm thought that was a good idea so he stretched out beside the young woman and went to sleep almost instantly.

He was awakened by a loud knock at his door. Longarm sat up and studied the young woman. Tiger was sleeping curled up in the nook of her right arm and they both appeared to be doing fine.

Longarm closed his bedroom door and went to see who was knocking. When he opened the door, it was his boss, Marshal Billy Vail, and he looked pretty unhappy.

"Custis. It's *noon*. We had an important meeting this morning at ten. When you missed it and didn't show up all morning, I got worried and decided to come and see if

15

you're all right. And, from the looks of you, I'd say that you're *not* all right."

"I'll live," he said, knuckling the sleep from his eyes.

Billy went over to the kitchen table and saw the two coffee cups. He frowned with disapproval. "Don't tell me," he said without trying to hide his sarcasm. "You picked up some two-bit whore last night, got drunk, and bedded her. And that's why you overslept and look like you've been dragged through a ragged knothole. Now, you're swilling coffee trying to get sober."

"That's not the way of it, Billy. Not the way of it at all."

He folded his arms across his chest. While Longarm was tall, Billy was short and stocky. He said, "I'm listening."

Longarm told his boss about the night before and about the woman sleeping in his bed . . . a woman beaten so savagely that she could not even remember her name. Longarm wasn't a man to ramble on with his words, and there was so much anger in his voice as he explained that Billy knew immediately Longarm was telling the truth and was filled with fury.

"I'm sorry," Billy said. "And you took the baby to the mortuary last night?"

"Yeah."

"Then whoever did this is going to either go to prison for a long, long time . . . or else hang."

"If a judge won't sentence him to death, then I'll kill him myself," Longarm vowed.

"Now you know you can't do that," Billy said, looking worried. "Sit down. Any coffee left in that pot?"

"I expect so."

"Then pour us some and let's talk about this mess your cat got you into last night."

Longarm did as he was asked. "We can talk, Billy. But the fact of the matter is that the girl has a serious head injury and can't remember who attacked her and her baby. Why, she can't even remember her own name."

"Hmm." Billy tried some of Longarm's coffee and nearly choked and spit it out. "Kee-rist this is strong!"

"Yep. Way I see it, you can water it down, but you can't water it up. Billy, you don't have to drink it, damnit."

"Take it easy," Billy said, his eyes tracking to the window. "Looks like the storm is letting up a little. We can ask around this neighborhood and see if anyone knows a young woman with a baby who's missing. Did you ever see her before in this neighborhood?"

"No." Longarm sipped his coffee thoughtfully. "Before she was beaten so badly, she was probably rather attractive. So, if she was from around here, chances are that I would have recognized her."

"That's probably true," Billy said. "And she had no identification on her?"

"Nothing." Longarm wondered if he ought to have a cigar. He felt restless and irritable. "Billy, the young lady was left to die under a wet mattress out in the back alley," Longarm said bitterly. "Whoever put her and that baby there didn't hold them any higher than trash!"

Billy pushed his coffee aside. "You know, Custis, this is a job for the local authorities. You're a federal marshal, and I have an assignment in Arizona that you need to handle. The girl should be in a hospital right now with doctors examining her. Not here in your apartment."

"When I told her she would be taken to a hospital," Longarm replied, "she damn near went crazy on me. So I thought she might stay here a day or two. Dr. Lander will be coming to see her pretty soon. And if I could take a few days off then . . ."

"Custis, that meeting you missed this morning was about the murder of the newly elected Governor Benton of

Arizona. The man was murdered a week before he was to be sworn into office. The people in Arizona are furious and there have been riots in Prescott. The local authorities there are either incompetent or indifferent. Hell," Billy scoffed, "they might even be behind Benton's murder for all I know."

Longarm had been to Arizona on a case only three months earlier. A bad case down in Yuma during the most terrible heat of summer. He wasn't eager to return to Arizona anytime soon. "Billy, can't you send someone else from the office?"

"Sure I can," Billy admitted, "but I won't. You're the best man by far for the job. Custis, don't quit on me now when everything is coming apart in Arizona and my own superiors are hounding me like mongrels on a meat bone."

"But . . ."

"The girl in your bedroom—whoever she is—will be well taken care of," Billy promised. "I'll personally take over the case and make sure that whoever beat her and caused the death of her baby is found and prosecuted to the full extent of our law."

"When do I have to leave for Arizona?"

"Today on the afternoon train."

"No," he said. "I'll leave tomorrow."

Billy started to protest. "Damnit, Custis, you don't—"

"Billy, that's the best that I can do!" Longarm thundered. "Why?"

Longarm looked through the doorway into his bedroom, feeling guilty for losing his temper and shouting at Billy, who was not only his boss but also one of his closest friends. "I need today at least to see if I can track down whoever did this to that woman. If I don't at least give it a try—and by that I mean at least stay here in Denver until tomorrow afternoon's train leaves—then my mind won't be able to focus on the problem in Arizona."

"Shit," Billy whispered, getting up from his chair and starting to pace back and forth in the small living room. "I'm gonna catch hell when I tell my bosses that you won't be on today's train out of town."

"Then lie to them," Longarm suggested. "Tell 'em I did leave on the train today. They won't know the difference."

Billy's jaw tightened and his fists clenched at his sides.

Longarm added, "Billy, one day more or less won't matter concerning what happened in Arizona. How long has it been since Benton was murdered?"

"A week. No, ten days. We gave the locals that long to figure it out, but they failed."

"Then one day more won't make any difference there, but it might make all the difference here in Denver when it comes to catching whoever beat that girl nearly to death."

"All right," Billy said, his shoulders slumping with resignation. "You've made a good argument for the delay."

Longarm almost smiled. "So you'll tell your bosses that I've left town today?"

"No," Billy said. "I can't lie. I'll tell them that . . . that you're ill. That you caught a bad head cold and have a fever, but that come hell or high water you are leaving for Arizona on tomorrow's train."

"Sounds good." Longarm stood up and stretched. "Billy, I need a small favor."

"What now!" Billy snapped with irritation.

"I need you to send one of the women from the office over here to watch over our mystery woman for a while. I'm going to canvass the neighborhood and see if anyone saw or heard anything last night concerning what happened in that alley."

"All right. I can send Samantha. She isn't worth a damn at anything but gossiping around the office anyway."

"Samantha will talk our girl into her grave," Longarm said in objection. "How about Mrs. Clara Waite?"

"My own personal secretary?"

"Yeah," Longarm said. "Clara is much better. She'll know how to take care of the girl until we can figure out what should be done for her."

Jaw clenched, Marshal Billy Vail nodded in reluctant agreement. He went to the bedroom door and glanced in at the girl, then came back out into the kitchen, his face pale with rage. "Custis," he said, "I don't think I've ever seen a woman beaten so badly. Take *two* days if you need them to find her assailant before you head off to Arizona."

"Thanks," Longarm said with a tight smile. "I ever tell you that you've got a good heart, boss?"

"No, and I don't want to hear that crap now," Billy snapped. "Just find that sonofabitch that did that girl so wrong. And when you get your hands on him, Custis, beat the living shit out of him before you drag him off to jail."

"My pleasure," Longarm said grimly as he reached for his hat, gun, and holster.

Chapter 3

Mrs. Clara Waite arrived within the hour to find Longarm pacing back and forth in his small living room. He was wearing his usual flat-brimmed, snuff-brown hat, a brown tweed suit and vest, blue gray shirt with a shoestring tie, and low-heeled army boots made of fine cordovan leather. At six four and with broad shoulders, Deputy Marshal Custis Long cut quite a strikingly handsome figure.

Mrs. Waite, however, gave him only a passing glance as she looked around and asked, "Where is the poor girl?"

"In my bedroom."

"In *your bedroom*! Good grief, that's certainly no place for a respectable lady."

"She might not be so respectable, Clara. Anyway, it's the best place for her right now," Longarm countered. "She'll be taken to the public hospital in a few hours . . . providing this storm lets up."

Clara Waite clucked her tongue disapprovingly and rushed into the bedroom. Hand flying to her mouth in shock, she breathed, "Dear God, I hope this poor waif survives. Why, someone beat her to within an inch of her life."

"Dr. Lander attended to her last night and he should be

coming around any time now. He seems to think that she'll make it, but the young woman has amnesia due to a severe concussion. She can't remember anything other than she had a baby."

"Tragic," Clara whispered into her cupped hands. "Absolutely tragic."

"I'm going out to see if I can find someone who knows who she is and who might have done her so wrong," Longarm explained. "I might not be back before she's taken to the hospital."

"I'll take good care of her," Clara said, back stiffening. "Just go find the man who did this."

"I'll try."

Longarm hitched his gun up a little under his overcoat. It was a double action Colt Model T .44-40 and it rode on his left hip, butt forward because he preferred a cross draw. He also had a mean double-barreled derringer of the same caliber that was cleverly attached to his gold watch chain instead of the usual fob. This derringer had saved his life many times when he'd pretended to check the time on his Ingersoll railroad watch, but instead pulled the deadly little pistol out to kill an enemy by surprise.

"Write me a note if you and the girl are gone when I return," Longarm said, going out the door. "I'll want to talk to her when she's fully conscious."

The rain was still falling, but not as hard. Longarm stepped outside the door of his apartment and considered where he should begin the search. He frowned for a moment and then he headed off down the street without any real idea where he was going.

At the street corner he met a couple huddled under an awning waiting for a hack. Longarm questioned them about the girl in his apartment, not expecting or receiving

22

any information. He stopped in at a ladies hat shop and described the young woman, but again learned nothing. Same result at a yardage and fabric shop popular among ladies. Two local pubs and two whiskies got him nothing except blank stares then sympathetic comments.

"This isn't working," he said to himself as he stuffed a cheroot into the corner of his mouth and stood just inside a doorway.

Then he had an idea. Maybe the girl had seen a doctor about having her baby. Longarm knew all the local businesses in this neighborhood and also its professionals so he headed off toward downtown. There were four or five good doctors on West Colfax Avenue who specialized in the health care of pregnant young women. Perhaps one of them had recently treated the woman he'd found last night and even delivered her baby before it died.

The first doctor knew nothing and was abrupt and dismissive, but the second one that Longarm visited had something of great interest to say after closely listening to Longarm's description of the mysterious woman.

"I can't be certain," Dr. Macklin said, pulling at his goatee and adjusting his spectacles, "but the lady you've described just might be one of my associate's more . . . more *troubling* patients.

"What do you mean?"

"My associate, Dr. Wilson, described a very unusual case to me last week. Unusual and extremely disturbing."

"Go on," Longarm urged.

Dr. Macklin was in his forties, slender and scholarly looking. His skin was so fair that you could see the blue veins in his temple and across his delicate hands. He tugged a little more at his thin goatee and continued. "It was last Thursday, or perhaps Wednesday. Yes, definitely Wednesday and in the morning. Hank—excuse me—Hank

23

is my associate, Dr. Wilson, who received a young woman escorted by a well-dressed but rude man who would not provide his name or state the nature of his relationship to the pregnant woman he had brought to our office. This young woman was very upset and crying. She was, according to Hank, only days from having her baby."

"Did you see the woman?"

"No," Macklin said, "I did not. I was attending to another patient at the time, yet I could not help but hear the sobbing and unmistakable hard words spoken to Hank."

"What 'hard words'?" Longarm demanded.

"From what I later learned, the man wanted the woman to lose the baby."

"Abort it?"

"Exactly. And, of course, that was absolutely out of the question for obvious reasons."

"One being it would quite likely also kill its mother."

Macklin nodded. "You are correct, Marshal Long. The argument continued and after about ten minutes the man and woman left . . . she still sobbing. As soon as I could, I went to see my associate and he was extremely disturbed by the encounter. He told me that the woman was unwell and underfed."

Longarm leaned in closer. "This is important. Did your associate, Dr. Hank Wilson, happen to see any scarring on the young woman? Any evidence of mistreatment or even beating?"

"Yes, he did," Macklin said without hesitation. "Even though no examination was given, my associate did observe scarring that was indicative of severe abuse."

"Where?"

"On her arms when he tried to take the young woman's pulse."

"Anywhere else?"

"Yes," Macklin said. "When the young woman removed her coat, my friend saw scarring on her neck."

"What happened to the couple?"

Macklin shrugged. "The man was furious when he learned that no abortion would be performed by any reputable doctor in this town because it would result in death. So he actually dragged the young woman sobbing out of our office and disappeared."

"Doctor, I badly need a name," Longarm said. "Of either party. Did they sign in or . . ."

"Well, they had to sign in," Macklin said. "It's required of all our new patients."

Longarm felt hope rising in his chest. "Where is the sign-in record?"

"I'll get it for you," Macklin replied. "Do you really think that the woman you told me about and the one that my associate saw so briefly are one and the same?"

"I'd almost bet my badge on it, Doctor."

Macklin led Longarm into a reception room where there was a large book very much like the kind that guests had to sign in upscale hotels at the registration desks. Dr. Macklin thumbed through the pages until he came to the Wednesday past and he studied the first entries of that day.

"Well, well," he said, looking disappointed. "Either it's a very large coincidence or you've run up against an obvious lie and not a very creative one."

Longarm saw the name that Macklin was pointing to with his pale finger: "Mr. & Mrs. John Smith."

"Damn!" Longarm hissed, feeling all his hopes being dashed.

"I'm very sorry, Marshal."

"Is there anything else they might have left to help me find them?" Longarm asked. "Anything at all."

"I'm afraid not, unless . . ."

25

"Unless what?"

"Unless they paid for our services in some manner other than cash or they required a receipt."

"Could you check?"

"Certainly."

"And is Dr. Wilson in today?"

Macklin glanced up at a wall clock with a swinging brass pendulum. "As a matter of fact, Hank should be arriving any minute."

"Good," Longarm said. "Because, right now, he's the only hope I have of finding out who the woman that I found last night almost dead is and who brought her here to abort her baby."

Longarm had only to wait ten minutes before a rather jaunty young man in a fine suit hurried inside shaking rain off his umbrella. He looked at Longarm and said, "Perhaps you are here by mistake? I specialize in the fairer sex, thank you very much."

Longarm had been sitting in the man's waiting room with two other women, both obviously pregnant. He came to his feet and discreetly showed Wilson his badge, whispering, "Doctor, I need only a few moments of your time on a very important matter."

The physician's demeanor changed in the blink of an eye and his smile died. "Of course. But as you can see, I have patients waiting and more will soon be arriving so I do hope this will be brief."

"It will be," Longarm promised.

Longarm was led into a small and cluttered medical office and the door was closed behind him. Wilson removed his coat and hat and hung them on a hat rack, then turned to Longarm and said, "Please tell me what I can do for you that you think is so important on such a miserable, stormy day."

Longarm repeated the story he'd already told many

times that morning. Dr. Wilson listened intently and grew slightly pale when Longarm described the mysterious woman and the cruel circumstances surrounding the death of her newborn.

"Describe the young mother more fully," Wilson said stoically.

When Longarm had finished his description and what had happened to her, the doctor said, "That's her, all right. I had a bad feeling about the poor woman and her unborn child and now I see that my instincts were correct."

"She has a severe concussion and can't remember anything. Do you know her name?"

"They signed into our office as Mr. and Mrs. John Smith."

"I'm sure that was not their real names."

"No," the doctor agreed. "But I do remember he called her Dilly."

Longarm frowned. "An unusual name."

"I thought so. Could be short for Delia."

"Could you describe the man for me?"

"Tall as you. Not as thick. Handsome. Rude and overbearing. Well dressed. I saw the butt of a pearl-handled derringer in his vest pocket."

"Clean shaven?"

"No. He wore a neatly trimmed mustache and beard. Black as night. He had brown, close-set eyes and . . ."

"And what?" Longarm prodded.

"They were vacant. Utterly lacking in compassion for the young woman or what I assumed was his unborn child."

"Can you tell me anything else that might help me find him?"

Wilson managed a smile. "I can, indeed."

"What?"

"I have seen this man at several recent social occasions. He frequents the horse track and the higher social circles in

27

our city. I last saw him at a party thrown by none other than the Buckinghams."

"I've heard of them, but never met them."

"They are extremely wealthy . . . but fine and generous people. They made their fortune on the Comstock Lode in Nevada. Anyway, this man you are seeking was their guest at a recent party I attended. And, I will tell you, he seemed to be quite a popular figure."

"But you didn't see Dilly there?"

"No."

"Can you tell me where I can find the Buckingham residence?"

"Of course." Dr. Wilson drew a quick map and even gave Longarm the address. "It's less than a mile from here. Huge brownstone mansion on a knoll. You can't miss it."

Longarm folded the paper up and slipped it into his pocket. "Is there anything else you can remember? Anything at all that you can tell me about this man?"

"Only that he is without soul or conscience. And, as I learned from his boorish reaction to my words, he is quick to anger. "If you find him, Marshal, you'd better take care."

Longarm smiled coldly. "*When* I find him, he is the one who had better be careful. Because I will not give him any quarter nor will I show him any mercy should he become violent or even verbally abusive."

The doctor nodded. "If I can help the young woman in any way, please know that I will be happy to do so—gratis. It's the least that I can do, and she was very sweet and gracious despite her desperate circumstances."

"I'll tell her that. She is being taken to our public hospital this afternoon."

"What a pity she can't go to Saint Joseph's Hospital, where she would be treated far more favorably."

"She'll survive," Longarm said. "I may not yet know

her true name, but I do know that she is strong and courageous."

Dr. Wilson found one of his business cards and scribbled a note on the back of it. "When you go to the Buckingham mansion, please tell them that it was I that sent you, and give them this card. It might help during your interview."

Longarm studied the card. Dr. Wilson had written, *Please help Marshal Long in any way you can. Yours, Hank.*

"I get the impression from your note that you know the Buckinghams rather well," said Longarm.

"I do. They are soon to be my in-laws. I am engaged to be married to their only daughter next month."

"Then congratulations are certainly forthcoming," Longarm said, shaking the man's hand.

"Again, be very careful. I sensed that this man is clever *and* deadly."

Longarm just nodded. Dr. Wilson wasn't telling him anything he did not already know.

Chapter 4

Longarm had no trouble finding the Buckingham mansion. With its sweeping front porch and marble pillars, it was even more impressive than described by Dr. Wilson. It was a two-story home and when Longarm rang the bell, he was reminded of how rich some people were compared to the working class and the poor.

He waited for quite some time at the door and it was finally opened by a very beautiful woman in her early forties wearing a pink chiffon gown and matching slippers. She held a glass of champagne filled to the brim. Over the expensive perfume, Longarm could smell the strong scent of liquor on her breath. When she spoke, her words were a little slurred.

"Good day, handsome sir," she said in greeting, raising her glass up between them and taking a sip. She licked her red lips and asked, "Have we met before?"

"No."

"Pity, that." She shrugged. "Oh well, we are meeting now, aren't we?"

"Yes, we are," Longarm replied, his eyes traveling past the woman down a long hallway hung with expensive gilt-framed pictures and impressive statues. "My name is Custis Long. Deputy Marshal Custis Long."

Her blue eyes widened with surprise that quickly transformed into amusement. "Don't tell me why you are here, Marshal Custis Long. I want to guess."

In his line of work Longarm had met all sorts, and this lovely and obviously tipsy lady was certainly one of the most interesting. "All right, ma'am, go ahead and guess."

She grabbed his sleeve with her free hand and pulled him inside the mansion and then closed the door, sloshing champagne on the floor. "Poor marshal, did you have to wait long before I arrived at the door?"

"Not too long. I was beginning to think that perhaps no one was at your home today."

She gave him what he suspected was a well-practiced pout. "The maid and butler have the day off. My husband . . . well, he *always* has his day off. And myself?" She giggled. "I am celebrating because I'm completely alone."

Longarm was bewildered. "And why would you celebrate that, Mrs. Buckingham?"

Her eyes narrowed and her lips formed a thin line. "If you must know, it's because my husband is a philandering bastard and my butler and maid are insufferably boring."

"And what about your daughter?"

"Oh, you know about her, do you?"

The woman was leading Longarm down the hallway into a room with an ornately carved bar backed by a mirror so big and extraordinary that Longarm thought it must have come out of an Italian castle. The room was filled with overstuffed furniture and there was an enormous bearskin rug on the polished wooden floor along with the mounted heads of several African big-game animals.

"Have you ever tasted France's best and most expensive French champagne, Marshal Long?"

"Not for at least a week," he deadpanned, wondering where this conversation was leading and how he could steer it back in the right direction.

"Well, then you shall!" she said, refilling her glass and then filling one for Longarm. "Drink up, Marshal Custis Long, because life is short and not so very sweet."

Longarm drank the champagne and then he smacked his lips with satisfaction. He had never tasted anything so fine.

"You like it?" she asked, looking pleased.

"The best I've ever tasted."

"Then drain that glass and let's have another."

Longarm thought that was a wonderful idea. Two glasses would not affect his thinking and he knew he would never again have the pleasure of drinking such nectar.

"Mrs. Buckingham," he said, "I *am* here on business."

"I'm sure you are," she said with a slightly lopsided smile. "You've come to tell me about my husband. He's been shot to death in some married man's bed while copulating with the wife in a very unnatural position."

Longarm blinked with surprise. "No. That's not it."

"What a shame," she said, looking sincere. "One of these days Reginald is going to be shot to death in someone's bed other than his own and he'll deserve it. I was rather hoping it was today."

Caught off guard by her candor and needing a few moments to collect his thoughts, Longarm appraised his splendid surroundings. "Mrs. Buckingham," he said, finally turning back to the woman, "I'm not here to discuss your marital problems and the infidelities of your husband. I'm here because I'm seeking out a man that may have committed a terrible crime."

"What nature of crime?" she asked, her smile slipping.

"I'd rather not say. The man I seek used the name John Smith."

33

Her eyebrows shot up. "That's entirely unimaginative."

"I take your answer to mean you have never met a John Smith."

"That's correct."

"Mrs. Buckingham, I think you have met this individual. He was at a party you held recently." Longarm described the man, then asked, "Can you tell me who he really is?"

"Oh, yes. Actually, I might." A sly smile formed on her lips. "But it will cost you something in return."

It was Longarm's turn to be surprised. "And what would that be, Mrs. Buckingham?"

"You really must call me Alicia. That's my name."

"Yes, but . . ."

"Drink up, Marshal."

Longarm didn't know where this conversation was headed and he was determined to get back to the point of his visit. "Perhaps we've both had enough to drink so early."

"Not nearly enough." Alicia raised her glass to him and he met her toast when she said, "To our . . . our arrangement. May it be mutually rewarding."

"What 'arrangement' are we talking about?"

Alicia Buckingham smiled coyly. "Lucky, lucky man, you're just about to find out."

Longarm had not a clue what she was talking about until the beautiful woman unbuttoned her silk gown to expose a pair of large, still firm breasts. "You've had the best champagne in the world, now you are about to have the best lovemaking."

Longarm nearly dropped his glass and retreated a step. "Mrs. Buckingham! What . . . What the hell is going on here?"

"Oh," she said, giggling and slowly undressing herself fully. "It's not what is going on . . . it's what's coming off."

"But . . ."

"Shhh," she whispered. "My husband is, at this very moment, screwing someone he is old enough to have fathered. And I just love the idea that . . . at the very same moment, I'm going to be screwing the handsomest lawman I've ever laid eyes upon."

Longarm gulped down his champagne and stared at Alicia's body. She was tall, slender, and stunning. Furthermore, despite the fact that he was here strictly on business, Longarm felt his passion and manhood rise.

"I really need to find out who John Smith really is," he said, his voice lacking conviction.

"You will," she purred, "if you satisfy me *completely*."

"And that's the arrangement?"

"That's it," she said, throaty laughter in her voice. "So, do you agree to the arrangement . . . or not?"

Longarm licked her taut nipples. "We have an arrangement, Alicia. Where is the closest bedroom?"

"We're not doing it on a bed," she told him as she began to unbuckle his gun belt and then his trousers. "We're going to make wild and passionate love right here on this thick bearskin rug."

The bearskin was huge and glossy. Longarm guessed it came from a trophy-sized grizzly or maybe one of those Alaskan giants that Longarm had heard was so prized by wealthy hunters.

"Why do it on the bearskin?" he asked as she knelt down before him.

She cradled his sack as if weighing it like a pouch of prospector's gold dust. "Because my husband, the philandering sonofabitch, loves to screw young women on this rug and I've caught him doing it more than once. So this is payback for him and pleasure for you and me."

Longarm took a sharp intake of breath as Alicia took

him into her mouth and began sucking on his big, stiff root. In moments, he knew that she was good . . . actually far better than good. The rich woman was amazing with her mouth and the way her tongue was able to massage Longarm until he was panting with desire.

"Ugh," he groaned. "You *really* know how to do this!"

"I learned at an early age and I've made it my business to keep in practice . . . but not on my husband. His carrot is so tiny and unworthy of my talent that I have to find men like you to keep in good practice."

Longarm moaned with pleasure and when he tried to pull back for a moment, she seemed to swallow him . . . rooting him to the bearskin like a tall statue.

"Enough for now," he gasped, finally pushing her back before he exploded. "It's your turn."

Longarm lowered Alicia onto the bearskin and began kissing her heaving breasts and then he inched lower and lower until he was devouring her honey pot. Alicia thrashed with ecstasy and when she finally began pleading for him to take her, Longarm jammed his big root into Alicia's juicy wetness and began pumping, but very slowly.

Somewhere down the hallway a great clock chimed over and over as they made agonizingly delicious love on the thick bearskin rug.

"You are even better than I've dreamed of having," she moaned at one point. "You are my ultimate fantasy lover!"

Longarm was also fulfilling his favorite fantasies as he slowly, expertly brought the rich and beautiful Mrs. Buckingham to a point of incoherent babbling and then a shuddering climax that was like a small earthquake. The woman screamed so loud that the sound of it echoed up and down the vast marble hallway and Longarm was grateful that the hired help had this day off as he plunged wildly, spewing reservoirs of his seed up into her heaving, clutching, and

36

eager womb. And he didn't stop until she went limp and her shuddering became a soft tremble.

"Custis," she said, breathing and looking up into his eyes with fresh tears, "you are a magnificent specimen of manhood. Even beyond magnificent."

"And you are my equal at lovemaking," he said honestly as he started to climb off.

"No, wait just a few moments longer," she pleaded, wrapping her long legs around his waist and holding him in tightly. "It still feels so wonderful."

Longarm pushed up on his arms and said, "I hate to end the moment, Alicia, but will you finally tell me who the man is that I need to find and arrest?"

"Yes, I will tell you anything. Anything you ask, if only you will promise me that this is not the last time we make love."

"Maybe you and your husband will make peace before then."

"Never," she said, voice hardening as she unwrapped him. "The little bastard is hopeless. He inherited all his money, you know. And without it I would never have given the little shit a second glance."

"Then why not leave him?"

Alicia laughed, but it wasn't a nice sound. "Because his lawyers would make sure I was penniless. And I've come to love my extravagances too much to go back to being poor. My weakness, I know. But I can live with that and the occasional pleasures I find in life. Pleasures like you, Custis, darling. Now, will you promise this isn't the end for us?"

"All right. I promise we'll do it again. On this rug, if you prefer."

"Oh, I certainly do prefer."

"Good," Longarm said. "Now, who is the man that I described and goes by the alias of John Smith?"

Alicia sighed and then rolled him off her. But instead of rising, she lay still, legs spread wide apart, and Longarm saw the smooth muscles of her flat belly contract. "What are you doing?" he asked.

"I'm leaking us all over my husband's bearskin rug, of course."

"But . . . but why?"

She giggled. "I don't think you'd understand, but any other woman who has been so often cheated upon would instinctively know the answer."

Longarm pulled on his pants and got dressed. He noticed that Alicia had produced a large wet stain on the bearskin and it amused him that most of it was his seed.

"All right," he said when he helped Alicia to her feet. "Now I want to know his real name."

"The young man you've described can be none other than Jim Brady, although even that might be an alias."

"What do you know about Brady?"

Alicia laughed and went to pour herself another glass of champagne. "I know that he isn't hung nearly as long between the legs as you are and that his lovemaking is a distant second to yours."

Longarm had to laugh. "That's flattering, but irrelevant."

"Not to me."

"What does Brady do for a living and where can I find him?"

"He is a gambler and a ladies' man. A con artist who has neither morals nor money, but does have looks and a devilish charm in spades. You can often find him at the racetrack downtown."

"The races aren't being held this month," Longarm said. "And I can't wait until next month. I need to find him today."

"Then I would look for him at Clancy's Betting Parlor.

38

He likes to spend his afternoons there . . . or so I'm told. You could probably find him there right now."

"Then I'd better be on my way," Longarm said, buckling his gun belt.

"Be careful, Custis Long. Jim Brady has the reputation of being an expert marksman and good with a knife."

"Thanks for the warning."

"Come back to me when you can. I won't soon forget you."

Longarm paused in the doorway. "Alicia, I'm not a man to give advice unless asked for, but . . ."

"Don't say anything," she said quietly. "I know what you want to tell me and I've heard it before from a few other good men."

He shrugged, knowing he would probably never see this complicated, tragic, and yet beautiful woman again. "All right then. Good-bye."

"I won't show you to the door, Marshal Long." And then without another word, she pulled her dress around her and went to get a fresh bottle of champagne.

Chapter 5

Longarm had been to Clancy's Betting Parlor in years past when he'd had to arrest Clancy for beating one of his unruly customers with his polished wooden Irish shillelagh. Although now in his early seventies, Clancy O'Toole was still big and strong. The man he had beaten had never fully recovered from the blows and had suffered permanent brain damage. The last Longarm had heard, the poor victim was still wearing diapers and drooling like a rabid dog. The victim's relatives had brought suit against Clancy O'Toole and won a large financial settlement, but Longarm doubted that any of it would ever be collected out of fear of retribution.

Everyone in Denver knew that Clancy O'Toole was a hard man and so were most of his regular Irish friends and bettors. In Clancy's mind, if you weren't from the "old sod of Ireland" you weren't worthy of his attention.

Now, Longarm paused outside the door of the betting parlor and checked his weapons one more time. He was sure that Jim Brady was Irish and so arresting the man and taking him out of Clancy's Betting Parlor and tossing him in jail was not going to be the least bit easy.

Inside, he could hear the Irish and their ribald, high-pitched laughter. Longarm decided the first thing he would do would be to go directly to Clancy O'Toole and quietly explain why he needed to arrest Jim Brady. Clancy was hard, but a recounting of how Brady had left a young woman and her newborn in a pile of alley rubbish might convince the Irishman to cooperate in the arrest.

Pushing open the door, Longarm stepped inside, sweeping the room with his eyes, but the room was dim and thick with bluish smoke. There were perhaps a dozen men inside, roughly half at the gambling tables and the rest drinking imported Irish beer and whiskey at the bar. Clancy's customers were not poor—the Irishman refused to serve inexpensive spirits not fermented or distilled in Ireland.

Clancy, as usual, was serving drinks, telling jokes, and smoking his briar pipe. Longarm went over to the bar and looked around for Jim Brady. It didn't take long to find the man he believed to be Brady. He was sitting at the betting table playing high-stakes poker. Longarm hid his disappointment. It would have been far easier to make his arrest if Brady had been drinking at the bar rather than sitting in the middle of a rousing poker game. But either way, Longarm was going to have his man, and as he discreetly watched Brady, he pictured Dilly's battered face and also that of the dead baby, who Brady had tossed on a trash heap to die.

"Well, well," Clancy O'Toole said, moseying over to Longarm with a disapproving scowl on his broad, pugnacious face. "If it isn't Marshal Custis Long. And what would the likes of you be doin' comin' into this honorable Irish betting and drinking parlor?"

"How about serving me one of your fine Irish beers?"

"Fair enough," Clancy said, pouring him one from a bottle. "Cost you six bits. I charge two bits extra for people I don't want to come in here."

"Fair enough," Longarm said, laying his money on the bar and taking a sip of brew that was bitter and sweet and altogether excellent.

There was a lot of yelling and laughing going on and Longarm was grateful that no one seemed to have overheard Clancy's remarks about him being a federal law officer. Longarm wanted to remain unnoticed until he grabbed Jim Brady and hauled him quickly and quietly out the door. Otherwise, some of these Irishmen, Clancy included, might take great offense and decide they needed to interfere on Brady's behalf. If that happened, Longarm had no doubt that he wouldn't get out of this place alive . . . at least not with his prisoner.

"Clancy," Longarm said in a low voice while easing down the bar as far removed from the others as possible. "I'm here to arrest Jim Brady and I need your help to do it."

Clancy's broad face was red and mottled. His nose had been broken from many a brutal fistfight and his eyes were red and watery from years of hard drinking. Now he removed his pipe from his mouth and spat into the dirty sawdust behind the bar. "And why on earth should I ever do that? Jim Brady is my friend and an Irishman. But you . . . You are not Irish and even worse, you're a fucking lawman!"

Several heads turned toward them, but no one seemed to have caught the full meaning of Clancy's hot words. Longarm was taller than Clancy and he stood up straight. "Jim Brady left a woman and her newborn baby to die in the alley behind my apartment. If I hadn't been out last night in that hard rain looking for Tiger—"

"For who?" the Irishman asked.

"My alley cat," Longarm explained. "But that isn't the point. I found this young woman and she was nearly beaten to death by Jim Brady and left to die. Her newborn child, *Brady's own child*, was left out in that cold rain and *did* die."

43

As hard as Clancy O'Toole was, the old man possessed a typical Irishman's sense of fair play and a big soft spot in his heart for the weaker sex along with helpless babies and children. Now, his ruined face softened as did his gravelly voice. "Are you sure of this terrible thing?"

"I am dead sure. The woman is still alive . . . although so badly beaten as to be nearly unrecognizable. She will testify in a court of law that it was Jim Brady who fathered her child and left it to die in wet garbage. Now I ask you, Clancy, what kind of a man would do such a thing to a young woman and his own spawn?"

O'Toole slowly revolved around to stare at Jim Brady, who seemed to be on a winning streak judging by his tall stacks of poker chips. O'Toole slowly shook his head and then turned back to Longarm. "You've accused Brady of a terrible sin, but I can't go against one of my own Irish. If I did that, I'd lose too many good friends and customers."

Longarm had been expecting that answer and had a ready reply. "Then just don't interfere when I go over there and arrest Brady. And if anyone at that poker table tries to stop me, make them have a quick change of heart. I'll do the rest and have Jim Brady out of here in minutes, provided I'm not forced to take on half of your customers."

O'Toole nodded his head with obvious reluctance and brought a Bible out from under the bar. "You'd better not have told me anything but the gospel truth here, Marshal Long."

"I swear that what I've told you is true."

"Put your hand on my Holy Bible and swear on it and on the name of your mother."

Longarm did both.

Clancy was disappointed, but resigned. "All right then, Marshal. But you'd better not have lied to me or to God. Because, if I find out that you told me a lie just to get Jim

Brady out of my place, then you and me will settle things. And when we do, your accursed blood will flow and you will have sent your soul to an everlasting and fiery hell."

"Clancy, I'm telling you the gospel truth. The mother, whose name is Dilly, is going to be sent to the public hospital today. She was so badly beaten she doesn't even know her real name. If you want, go to the public hospital and you'll see with your own eyes that I haven't lied or exaggerated about Jim Brady."

"I might just do that," O'Toole decided aloud. "Now do what has to be done. But don't kill the man or any of my customers."

"I'll try to take Brady peacefully," Longarm promised. "And I expect that won't be a problem—so long as no one else in this parlor interferes—especially you and your wicked Irish shillelagh."

"You have my word we'll all stay out of it," O'Toole promised, reaching under the bar and producing the knobby blackthorn cudgel that could bring even a draft horse to its knees with a single blow.

Longarm nodded in thanks and with no small measure of relief. With Clancy O'Toole's permission to make the arrest, things might even go smoothly.

"Here goes," Longarm said, pushing back from the bar and drawing his pistol from its holster but keeping it well hidden under his coat while using his left hand to pick up his glass of dark beer.

Hat tipped down, Longarm sauntered over to within ten feet of the poker table attracting no attention. Leaning against the wall, Longarm took a few minutes to study Jim Brady. The man was tall and handsome, probably in his late twenties, with a neatly trimmed black beard and mustache. Longarm couldn't see the pearl-handled derringer that the doctor had warned him rested in Brady's vest pocket, but he assumed it was there all the same. Brady also wore a six-gun on his right hip and Longarm caught sight of the bulge of a bowie knife on the man's left hip. All in all, Brady was extremely well-heeled.

"You lookin' to sit in on this game, mister?" Brady asked, suddenly turning his attention to Longarm. "Won't be long before a few of these gentlemen are broke and there will be an empty seat. I can always use some fresh money and blood."

Several of the losing players at the table laughed without humor. Longarm didn't laugh a bit. He pushed off the wall and drew his gun, pointing it at Jim Brady. "I'll pass on the game. But I'm a federal officer of the law and you are under arrest. Put your hands up high!"

Brady's face flushed with blood as his smile died. "I'm under arrest?" he gritted.

"That's right."

"For what?"

"For the murder of your infant son and the beating of a woman you call Dilly."

Brady's close-set brown eyes blinked rapidly and then his broad shoulders slumped, but not with resignation. "Well, well," he said, more to the men sitting at the table than to Longarm. "I've been accused of a terrible crime that I never committed. And now, this fool wants to arrests me."

"Not 'want'," Longarm corrected. "I *am* arresting you for murder and assault. Stand up slow and get those hands in the air now!"

Jim Brady was cool and collected. He smirked and pushed his chair back from the poker table with exaggerated slowness. Then, he grinned and glanced over at Clancy O'Toole standing behind his bar. "Clancy, are you going to let this sonofabitch just come into your place of business and do this to a fellow Irishman?"

"I am if what he's accusing you of is true."

"But damnit, it's not!" Brady exploded. He came to his feet, raising his hands only to his shoulders. "Gentlemen, this charge is a bald-faced lie. I've never beaten a woman in my life and I damn sure never fathered some bastard child by her!"

"Shut up and raise those hands higher," Longarm ordered, coming in closer to disarm Brady.

Brady yelled, "Fellow Irishmen, this is an Englishman with a badge and a lie! Help me!"

Longarm saw a movement out of the corner of his eye. He didn't want to turn from Brady, but someone might be drawing down on him so he had no choice.

A glass of beer smashed Longarm in the face and he desperately tried to swipe it away with his sleeve. But Jim Brady was on him before he could see the man and Longarm felt a sharp pain in his side and knew that Brady had stabbed him with the bowie knife.

Longarm tried to turn, but he was mobbed and driven to the floor.

"Run, Jim! Run!" someone shouted hoarsely. "We've got him down now so run!"

Longarm struggled valiantly to throw the men off, but he was helpless under their weight and he knew that he was losing blood.

"Get off that man!" O'Toole boomed. "Get away from him now or I'll be splitting your thick Irish skulls like melons!"

Suddenly the weight was gone and Longarm was rolled onto his back to stare up at Clancy O'Toole, who was bent over and looking down at him without mercy or pity.

"Can ya stand on your own two feet?" the big Irishman asked.

Longarm gritted his teeth and climbed erect with his

knees ready to buckle and blood trickling down his side and ringing in his ears from several hard blows to the head. He touched the knife wound and was relieved to discover that it wasn't a fatal blow. Nothing had been cut except muscle.

"Lawman, I'll get you a bottle of my best Irish whiskey . . . on the house," O'Toole said, hurrying over to his bar and slamming his shillelagh against the wall. "It'll fix you right up, Marshal!"

An old, short, red-faced Irishman handed Longarm his gun then pointed at the door. "Jim Brady would never have done what you accused him of, Marshal. We knew that and that's why we brought you down so that he could get away clean."

Longarm glared at all of them. "I could arrest the lot of you for obstruction of the law. But I'd only be dirtying the city jail and wasting my time. Does anyone care to tell me where Jim Brady lives?"

Blank faces. Not a word.

"Yeah," Longarm said bitterly as Clancy O'Toole handed him a full bottle of his best Irish whiskey. "I didn't think so."

"Marshal," one of the Irishmen said, "if I was you, I wouldn't be comin' back here to look for Jim again."

"I don't intend to ever come back here," Longarm said. "And just to set the record straight, I'm not an Englishman."

"You're not?"

"No. I'm . . . I'm a mongrel. A mixed-breed fella that has had more than his fill of you damned self-righteous Irish."

"Now, now, no cause for insults. Drink up, Marshal," O'Toole ordered while placing Longarm's hat back on his head. "It'll restore the blood that you're losin'."

Longarm uncorked the bottle and took a deep, fiery swig. It warmed him right down to his toes and cleared the pain and fogginess from his brain. It tasted so good and made him feel so much better that he took another long pull and then he looked around to see O'Toole and his Irishmen wearing broad smiles.

"No hard feelings there, Marshal," O'Toole said. "Let's all get drunk now and talk about this trouble you brought into my place."

Longarm wanted to kill every last one of them but instead he gritted, "I didn't bring in the trouble; Jim Brady did. And I'll find him, Clancy. I'll find him and then I'll invite every damn one of you Irishmen to his public hanging."

"Wouldn't be the first we'll have witnessed," one of the Irishmen said in a sad voice. "The English hanged an Irishman every day of the week back on the old sod and two on Sundays."

It was apparently a joke. Everyone roared. Everyone except Custis Long, who took another long swig of the Irish whiskey and staggered outside to find a doctor and then to find Jim Brady again.

Chapter 6

Longarm made his painful way over to Dr. Wilson, who cleaned the wound and used five stitches while Longarm explained what had gone so wrong at Clancy's Betting Parlor.

"You're lucky to have come out of that unsavory place with your life, Marshal."

"I guess I am," Longarm agreed. "I thought Clancy was good for his word, but someone hit me with a glass of beer and that was all that Brady needed to have full advantage. That aside, do you know how Dilly is?"

"She's doing as well as can be expected. However, I just learned that she can't be moved to the public hospital until the day after tomorrow. There are no available beds right now. I went over to your apartment to tend to her and she's pretty upset."

"She has every right to be. Doc, do you think she'll ever regain her memory?"

"I don't know. I'm hopeful that she will . . . but her brain has been badly injured. The good news is that she can still think and talk reasonably well. The bad news is that it will take weeks, possibly months, for her to fully recover from all the physical damage she's suffered."

"I'm going to get Jim Brady," Longarm said, gritting as the doctor applied a small bandage to the side of his head. "And the next time I have him in my gun sights, if he so much as twitches, I'll kill the rotten sonofabitch."

"I don't blame you a bit," the doctor said, finishing up his ministrations. "But what you need right now is rest."

"No rest for the wicked," Longarm said with self-deprecation. "I've got to be on the train leaving Denver tomorrow afternoon. I've got important business to take care of in Prescott, Arizona."

The doctor shook his head. "It'll have to wait a few days until I'm sure that you're well enough to travel."

"Tell that to my boss, United States Marshal Billy Vail."

"I will, if he asks. But this knife wound you suffered is quite serious. You can't be jostled and bumped around, or it could open and you might bleed to death. So you have to be still for at least the next few days."

Longarm just nodded, not sure what he would do tomorrow. "Doc, where is Dilly going to stay until they can take her to the hospital?"

Without looking up from his bandaging, Dr. Wilson said, "Marshal, how about your place?"

"Not a good idea."

"Well, I can't take her in and I don't know who can. Marshal, you found her and she keeps asking about you, which tells me that you might be the only one that she feels she can trust right now."

"But . . ."

"Custis, the woman is badly traumatized. She looks like death and doesn't want to be seen in public. She's afraid of her own shadow. And you know the interesting part?"

"What's that?"

"She asked me if you and her were married."

"No!"

"Yep," the doctor said, "and although I told her you were not her husband, she's convinced that you are. And the other thing is that she and your cat seem to have taken up quite a friendship."

"Tiger *likes* her?"

"Why wouldn't he?"

Longarm shrugged, feeling a bit betrayed. "No reason, Doc. It's just that I never saw Tiger take up with anyone other than myself."

"Maybe Dilly and Tiger forged a bond during that terrible storm out in your back alley. I can't explain it, Custis, but I'm truthfully telling you how it is right now. If you move that poor, frightened young woman and put her in an institution, I'm afraid that . . . Well, it could push her over the edge into insanity."

"Damn," Longarm whispered. "As if I don't have enough problems already."

"Go back to your apartment. I saw that you had almost no food in your icebox or pantry so I stopped by the grocery and paid them to send up some food. I also left some medicines for Dilly, but they will help you too."

"Why, that's mighty generous of you."

"No it isn't. I'm adding it to your bill."

"Oh."

Wilson smiled and chuckled. "Marshal, relax. I'm *kidding*. You've done a lot for the woman and now you both need to just rest and recover for a while."

"But . . . but, Doc," Longarm tried to voice his deep concern. "I don't know her and I darn sure don't know what to say to her."

"It'll come to you," Wilson counseled. "Just be yourself and whatever you do, for heaven's sake don't say or do anything that could frighten or upset her. Don't argue when she says that you're her husband and Tiger is her cat. Custis, this woman has lost her baby. She doesn't need to feel any more loss for a while. More disappointment could cause her permanent mental illness. It might send her flying over the brink into complete madness. All right?"

"All right."

Longarm was still trying to get a handle on all this as the doctor eased him out of the examination room and into the waiting room, which was full of pregnant ladies. When Longarm made his appearance, they all stared and then began to titter with hushed amusement.

They fell silent as Longarm glared at them and barged out through the front door.

"Listen," Longarm said as he stood in the doorway of his apartment talking in a hushed voice to Billy Vail. "Things have gotten a lot more complicated since we talked last."

"Yeah, I can see that," Billy said, peering through the doorway at Dilly and then back to Longarm. "You went to find the man who did this and got beat up and stabbed. Then this woman decided that you're her husband and you both own an orange tomcat. Now, you're trying to tell me that you can't go to Prescott as promised!"

Longarm lifted and then dropped his hands in a gesture of utter futility. "I'm sorry, Billy. Sometimes things don't work out the way they are supposed to through no fault of our own."

Billy pulled Longarm out into the hallway and shut the door so they could speak in private. "I've got a lot of pressure on me to send a man to Arizona and get to the bottom of Governor Benton's murder. Now I am not an unreasonable man . . . but you have to help me out here."

"The doc says that I must have a few days of rest. And besides, I want to take one last try at finding and arresting Jim Brady, the man who did this."

"The hell with Brady! He's a nobody. We've got an Arizona governor that was murdered. That's what we need to go to work on solving."

"What's this 'we' stuff?" Longarm asked. "Sounds like it's me or nobody. Why can't you send Deputy Ben Tucker? He's a smart and resourceful fellow and in Prescott he'll do the job right."

"Okay, I will," Billy spat. "I'll send Tucker instead of you. Does that make you happy?"

"Not especially," Longarm replied, "but I think it's a smart move. Tucker is a good lawman and he won't embarrass you or our department."

"Okay," Billy repeated, "Tucker it is. But if he has trouble or . . . or you know . . ." Billy stammered to silence.

Longarm understood Billy all too well. "You're trying to say that if Tucker either gets in bad trouble or gets killed, you want me to go next."

"Exactly."

"It's a deal," Longarm said. "But in the meantime, I need to rest and then spend a little time tracking down Jim Brady. You just took a good look at that girl, Billy. How can you expect me to walk out on Dilly when she's been through so much . . . even losing her newborn baby in the trash and rain?"

"Okay. Okay!" Billy said. "You're right. Stay here and help her for a few days and get your knife wound to healing."

"And get Jim Brady."

"Forget Brady! I'll ask the local sheriff to go after the man and lock him up on the charge of murder and assault."

Longarm sighed with disgust. "Billy, we both know that Sheriff Adams and his Denver deputies aren't fit to find their own asses."

"Yeah," Billy admitted. "I know. But everybody gets

55

lucky sometimes. Custis, just rest and be ready if I need you to jump on the train bound for Arizona."

"I'll do that," Longarm promised. "And Billy?"

"Yeah?"

"Say hi to the wife and kids for me."

"Will do," Billy said as he left.

Longarm closed the door and turned around to see Dilly gently stroking Tiger. The alley cat was resting in her lap and the damned thing was actually purring. Longarm again felt betrayed because he'd never seen Tiger purr around anyone except himself.

"Well," he said, going over and sitting in his favorite chair, "how are you feeling today?"

"Much better," Dilly said, although she didn't look better.

"That's good to hear," Longarm said, trying to think of something else to say to her but coming up blank.

Her lower lip began to quiver and Longarm knew that tears weren't far behind. "I'm so terribly sorry about our baby, Custis."

He started to remind her that it hadn't been *their* baby, then changed his mind. She looked so small and hurt that he just didn't have the stomach to risk upsetting her further. "Me too, Dilly."

"Where did you put all my clothes?"

"I . . . I guess they got lost. We'll find some more."

"All right," she said. "I don't really need many clothes. It's warm in here."

"Want me to open the window?"

"No, I'll be fine."

Dilly set Tiger on the floor and unbuttoned the heavy woolen shirt that Longarm had put on her to get her warm and dry. Her breasts, heavy with mother's milk, were a pleasant but troubling sight. Longarm tore his eyes away from them and went to stare out the window. He could see

56

the exact pile of rubbish and old ripped mattress where he'd found the pair only last night. It hardly seemed possible that so much had happened in less than twenty-four short hours.

"Custis?"

He turned to face her and those large, inviting breasts. "Yeah?"

"How long have we been married?"

Longarm took a deep breath. He just felt himself sinking into this situation deeper and deeper. "Not long," he said, vaguely.

"But at least nine months."

"Yeah."

"Thank goodness for that! I sure was hoping that you didn't marry me because you got me pregnant out of wedlock."

"No, Dilly. I surely didn't do that."

"Good. Did we have a nice wedding?"

"Swell."

She stroked the cat and it resumed purring. "I just wish that I could remember us meeting and falling in love. Making love." She started tearing up and then she said, "Custis, I know I look like a fright . . . but I'll look better soon. And then you'll want me again like a good husband should. Won't you, darling? Won't you?"

He groaned inwardly and just managed to nod.

She was buoyed by his response and wiped away the fresh tears. "I'll bet, when my face is nice and healed and your head and body are healed—when we're all healthy again and dressed up fine—then we'll make an absolutely smashing-looking couple together out in public."

Longarm had to grin despite what was going on inside his head. "You know, Dilly, I think we will at that."

"Come sit here beside me on the couch," she pleaded. "Hold me a little while."

The shirt was open, his eyes were glued to those breasts, and he was feeling as if he were falling into something that he might not be able to handle. "But what about Tiger?"

She lifted the cat and set him down on the floor. "Tiger knows that we love him. But right now, I need to feel your strong arms around me. I need that real bad, darling husband of mine."

Longarm lurched forward without any more hesitation. He didn't even try to resist her heartfelt plea. Dilly, or whatever her real name was, had already been put through hell and, for the time being, Longarm didn't have the heart to disappoint her in any way at all.

Longarm awoke in the deep, dark of night to feel Dilly touching his manhood and kissing his cheek. He reached over and gently cradled her battered face.

"Dilly, what are you . . ."

"I want you inside of me," she whispered.

"No! Dilly, we just can't do that."

"Please!" There was a desperation and urgency in her voice that shocked him.

"Dilly, listen. You're not well enough . . ."

"Gently. If you do it gently, we'll both be all right. I know that we will. But if you won't do it to me, then I'll understand because I am so beaten up and ugly right now."

"You're not ugly, Dilly."

"Then don't say anything more, Custis. Just take me gently and I'll tell you if it hurts too much."

She was stroking his manhood and Longarm hated himself for swelling up like a big salami. So he did as she asked and eased on top of Dilly and entered her just as gently as he possibly could.

"Does it hurt?" he asked, feeling almost overwhelmed by guilt.

"No," she said, hugging him around the neck and then wrapping her slim and shapely legs around his waist. "Darling husband, am I hurting your side wound?"

"Not that I can tell."

"Good." Dilly squeezed him, sighing with pleasure. "This is what I needed tonight so that I know you still love me, my dear husband. Please, please tell me that you love me."

Longarm felt her trembling with—with what? Hope? Fear? He couldn't risk saying the wrong thing and destroying Dilly.

"I do love you, Dilly. I really do love you."

She clung to him as if he were a rope suspending her from some terrible abyss. And then she began to move her hips and make sweet, easy love to Longarm in a way that he had never been made love to before.

Chapter 7

Longarm and Dilly awoke to a bright, sunshine-filled day. Longarm added a little extra water to his usual gut-buster boiled coffee and then fried some eggs and bacon. Dilly talked about the weather and how she was feeling much better.

"You'll be moved into the public hospital in a few days," Longarm told her. "As soon as they have an extra bed."

"But why would I want to do that?" She hurried over to him. "Custis, you're my husband and I want to stay right here with you."

Again, Longarm saw the sudden desperation in her eyes and again he backpedaled on the truth as he placed their breakfast on the table. "Eat up, Dilly. We can talk about this later."

"I want to talk about it right now. Why would you send me to a hospital when I'm so happy to be here with you and Tiger?"

Longarm couldn't come up with an honest answer so he said, "I'm a federal officer of the law, Dilly. And I'm probably going to have to travel all the way to Arizona."

"Where is that?"

"It's a long way off even on a train."

"I want to go with you."

At that moment, Tiger meowed, wanting either more food or more attention. "But who would take care of poor Tiger?"

She nodded with understanding. "Yes, you're right. I'd have to stay here with Tiger. Besides, I look so bad you'd be ashamed to tell people that I was your wife."

"I'd never be ashamed of you," Longarm said, meaning it. "And as for all those cuts and bruises on your face, they'll be healed before you know it and you'll be beautiful again."

"You promise?" she asked.

"I do." Longarm ate in silence for a few minutes and then said, "Dilly, I know that you don't remember much about your past, but does the name Jim Brady ring a bell?"

He could see that it did because Dilly dropped her fork on her plate and her face grew a shade paler.

"What can you tell me about the man?" Longarm asked softly because he knew he was treading on very thin ice.

"Why do you ask?"

Longarm could see hysteria rising in her blue eyes. She was, he feared, about to slip over the edge just as Dr. Wilson had predicted. "Never mind. Just . . . Just forget that I asked."

But Dilly was too upset to let it go. "Is Jim Brady an old friend of yours?"

"More like a new enemy," Longarm said, trying to keep the tone of his voice casual so as not to alarm her any more than he had already. "Jim Brady is the one that knifed me in the side. Being a law officer, I want to find and arrest him."

Longarm saw no sense in upsetting her further by explaining that Brady was the father of the dead child and the one who had also left her for dead. "Dilly, I was just hoping you might know where he lives."

Dilly focused hard on straightening her fork on her

plate, then said, "I *do* know where he lives. I don't know why I know . . . but I do."

"Can you tell me?"

"Yes." She concentrated hard and Longarm ached for the struggle she was mentally undertaking. Finally, Dilly said, "Mr. Brady lives in a fine hotel called the Dakota."

"I think I know where that is. On Fifteenth Avenue near the corner of Stout Street? Big, three-story building made of brick?"

"That's the one."

Longarm finished his eggs and picked up his coffee casually, asking, "Do you happen to remember Jim Brady's room number?"

"Why should I?"

"I was just hoping . . ."

She frowned with concentration. "It's number two zero four. Yes. I'm quite sure that's it."

Dilly couldn't say any more and began to cry. Longarm comforted her as best that he could and said, "Don't be upset. It'll be all alright."

"But why is this upsetting me so? Why am I crying? Is Jim Brady supposed to mean something to me?"

"I don't know," he lied. "But this question and so many others will be answered in their own good time. Don't try to force anything. Just . . . Just heal and start feeling good again."

Longarm finished his coffee. He quickly shaved and dressed in a new suit, shirt, and tie because yesterday's clothing had been ruined on the sawdust floor in Clancy's Betting Parlor when he went down. He put those clothes in a bag to go into the trash when he hit the street.

"I have to go out for a while," Longarm said. "Dr. Wilson will probably be around before long to check in and see how you're doing."

"He's a very nice young man. Is he married with children?"

"No, but he's engaged," Longarm answered. "Dilly, lock the door and don't open it unless it's the doctor."

"All right. Will you be gone all day?"

"Probably not," Longarm said, kissing her gently and then putting on his hat. "I'll try to return as soon as I can."

"Please do."

Longarm left her and hurried down the stairs to the street. He knew exactly where the Dakota was located and had even been inside its ornate lobby on a few occasions to buy a cigar or a newspaper. The Dakota rented by the day, week, or month and was high-toned and expensive, which told Longarm that Jim Brady must be winning big at poker.

"Well, today Brady is going to play his last hand and it's going to be snake eyes," Longarm said to himself as he headed briskly down the street.

When he arrived at the Dakota, Longarm removed the bandage from his head because the wound wasn't serious and he didn't want to attract any attention going through the lobby and up the stairs to Room 204. Because he was so tall and such a striking figure, Longarm did, however, catch the eye of the uniformed desk clerk who smiled widely and then beckoned him over.

"Are you arriving to register as our guest, sir?"

"Afraid not. I've come on business to see one of your guests."

"Which one would that be?"

"Jim Brady. Room two oh four."

"Ah, yes. Mr. Brady. Well, I haven't seen him leave yet and he usually has a Do Not Disturb Until Noon sign on his door so we don't bother him at this hour." The man shrugged. "Is Mr. Brady expecting you?"

"I doubt it."

"Then I'm afraid that you'll have to come back later."

"No I won't." Longarm showed the clerk his federal officer's badge and said, "I'll take a key to Mr. Brady's room."

"But—"

"This is *official* business. Don't make me cause a fuss. I'm sure your other guests don't need that, now do they?"

"Of course not, Marshal!"

The clerk hurried off and returned with the hotel spare key. "Please don't cause us any embarrassment, Marshal. Our guests expect—."

"I'm sure that they expect nice, peaceful surroundings," Longarm said in his most reassuring voice. "And, if possible, I'll try to keep things that way. Do you have a fire escape from the second floor?"

"Yes, sir. At the end of the hallway you'll see a sign. But it's a drop ladder and hasn't been used or even tested since the hotel was built almost twenty-five years ago. It's simply an emergency exit."

"Most fire ladders are," Longarm said as he pocketed the key and headed toward an impressive spiral staircase that would lead him to Brady's room.

At the second-floor landing, Longarm turned around and surveyed the lobby. Expansive and sparkling, the Dakota was indeed very impressive with massive crystal chandeliers, ornate furniture no doubt imported from Europe, a plush wine-colored rug that would have cost a fortune, a bubbling fountain, and a gift shop that sold East Coast newspapers and only the best liquor and cigars.

The luxury of the hotel only compounded Longarm's anger toward Jim Brady. How could such a man live in such opulence and then callously discard his wife or lover along with his newborn child in a garbage-strewn back alley? Longarm knew the answer to that question even as he headed down the hallway to Room 204. The answer was that only a monster without a shred of conscience or morality could do what Jim Brady had done to Dilly and her baby.

Longarm stopped at Brady's room and looked up and down the dim hallway. It was empty so he leaned forward, placing his ear against the door and listening. He hoped to hear the sound of loud snoring. That being the case, he would use his key and enter to subdue and then arrest Brady before the man was fully awake.

It would be easy.

Longarm listened, but heard no sound. He eased the key into the keyhole and turned it with just the faintest *click*. Then he pushed inside and looked around. The apartment was splendidly appointed. He was standing in the living room, and directly across from him was a set of windows overlooking the street toward the capitol building. Tall trees framed the window and it made a beautiful view.

But Longarm wasn't interested in the view. Tiptoeing forward, he turned left toward what he suspected was the bedroom. He was right. The bedroom was occupied—but not by Brady. Instead, a lovely blonde was fast asleep with her hair fanning out over a pillow.

Longarm swore silently to himself as he searched the other rooms and found them empty. Brady was gone.

He returned to the bedroom and roused the sleeping woman. She sat up with a shriek of surprise and fear. "Who are *you?*"

"Easy, miss. I'm a deputy United States marshal. And I'm looking for Jim Brady."

"He isn't here."

"I can see that, miss. *Where* is he?"

She wasn't fully awake enough to cover her breasts, and her hair was in her eyes. She blew the hair away and shook her head, muttering, "We had quite a night. Musta drank a full bottle of champagne on my own and—"

Longarm grabbed her by the arm, feeling a sense of overwhelming urgency. "Miss, never mind that. I have to find Jim Brady right away. Where the hell did he go!"

She moaned. "I don't like being awakened so rudely by a stranger, then being yelled at. Let go of me."

Longarm released the woman and folded his arms across his chest. "Miss, I need to know where Brady has gone."

"Why?"

"You don't need to know."

"Has he hurt someone again?"

Longarm nodded. "Now, are you going to help me or do you want to go down to the jail and—"

"All right! I'll help you. There's no need to be rude or threatening."

"Sorry, miss."

She sat up, realizing that her breasts were hanging out in the open. With a half smile and no attempt to feign modesty, she said, "Jim told me last night that he had some important personal business to attend to first thing this morning and that he'd only be gone an hour or two. He wrote down the address where he was going on a piece of paper. It's probably still resting on the armoire."

Longarm strode across the room to the armoire and snatched up the scribbled address, then stared at it.

"Holy shit!" he cried, feeling his stomach turn into knots.

"What's wrong now?" the woman demanded.

"This is *my* address!"

Longarm wheeled and bolted for the door. The blonde called out something that he did not wait around to hear. Jim Brady was going to Longarm's apartment and there was nobody home except sweet, defenseless Dilly.

Chapter 8

Dilly was lying on the bed, eyes closed and thinking about her Custis when she heard the knock on the door. Tiger, close beside her, stopped purring and jumped off the bed to hide under Longarm's favorite chair.

Given that Longarm had told her the kind doctor would come by to pay a professional visit, Dilly had found a pair of Longarm's pants to go along with one of his shirts. Both articles of clothing were ridiculously big and made her look like a ragamuffin. For the life of her, Dilly could not understand why there weren't any of her clothes in the closet. But, as Custis had promised, many things would be revealed as she began to remember.

The knock was loud and insistent. "Coming!" she called, trying to hitch up the pants so that they wouldn't fall off and embarrass both herself and the kind doctor. "Be right there!"

As she sort of stumbled toward the door, she did remember Custis warning her not to let anyone inside other than the doctor. But who would come other than he?

Dilly paused at the door and then she looked up and saw that there was a short chain and latch that would allow her to safely open the door just a mere crack. The knocking was getting even louder.

"Doctor, just a moment please."

She set the little safety chain in its latch and turned the bolt on the door. Pushing it open until it reached the allowance of the chain, she peered through the crack and then her eyes widened in revulsion. "You! Oh, no!"

If anything, Jim Brady was almost as shocked. "Dilly? What . . . Open the door! It's me, Jim."

Her hands started shaking and her knees went weak and began to buckle. Dilly's throat constricted and she squeaked, "I—"

"Open the damned door! It's me, Jim. Your love."

Dilly reached up toward the chain, her entire body shaking so hard she could barely stand erect. Then she started to remember something terrible and staggered back, still seeing Brady's angry face through the narrow door opening. "You . . . you . . ."

Brady suddenly realized that Dilly was going to leap forward and slam the door, so he did the only thing that he could and that was to beat her to the punch. Throwing his weight and shoulder into the door, he tore the latch free and pitched headlong into the apartment watching Dilly's face register stark terror.

He climbed off the floor and smirked. "Now you're starting to remember things, aren't you sweetheart?"

"Jim, you're the one that . . . You beat me and left me and our baby for dead in the rain!"

He closed the door and shot the bolt, then studied the damage he'd done with his fists. It was a pretty impressive beating by any standards.

"Jim, why?"

"You wouldn't agree to get rid of the baby and I sure wasn't going to marry you and support a family. Oh no!

You'd have tried to force me to do that and it would have ruined my standing in this town. I'd have been disgraced. I just couldn't let that happen, Dilly. I couldn't let you mess things up for me like they were messed up before."

She was retreating toward Longarm's window, obviously reliving the horror of her last beating at his hands. "My name is Delia . . . Delia *Hamilton.*"

"Very good," he said like a teacher to a small child. "And as long as you're starting to remember the past, do you know where we met?"

She blinked and then her lips formed a circle and she stammered, "Philadelphia. Yes! My father didn't approve of you so we ran off to get married and landed up here in Denver."

"Excellent," he said with his condescending smile. "Your family is quite wealthy, Dilly. I thought that I'd get fixed up for life, but your father did some checking around and . . . Well, he decided that I just wasn't quite up to snuff. Not quite in your upper, snobbish class."

Brady's voice suddenly hardened. "So I wound up with you and no money and a damned baby on the way. It was altogether a disaster, dear Dilly. And you wouldn't have that abortion or help fix the problem so I fixed it myself in the alley behind this building."

She reached out as if to hold him away from her. "Jim, please! Please don't hurt me any more."

Brady had a pair of kidskin leather gloves in his pocket and he slowly removed them from his jacket and pulled them on with exaggerated slowness, starting to enjoy himself. He had come to surprise and kill the marshal who was after him, but instead here was Dilly. Life sure was full of surprises.

"Where is Marshal Custis Long?" he asked quietly. "Has he gone to work today?"

She swallowed hard. "No. He . . . He said he'd only be gone a few minutes. He'll be right back, Jim. You'd better go now."

He shook his head and made a face. "I don't think so."

"Please go!"

Brady surveyed the humble and poorly furnished little apartment. "Not too impressive, Dilly. Not nearly as nice as your family's estate back in Philadelphia. An estate I thought I'd soon find a way to inherit."

She began to beg. "Jim, don't hurt Custis or me. Just go and I won't even tell him that you were here. I swear that I won't."

"Oh," Jim said softly, "you don't need to make such promises, Dilly. Because, the truth be known, you won't be able to tell anyone anything when I'm finished with you."

She backed up against the window.

He laughed. "Why Dilly my love! Do you like the view into that back alley where I thought you had died? Maybe you'd like to open that window all the way and jump out."

"No!" she screamed.

He took a step forward, tightening the leather glove on his right hand. "This time I won't mess things up, my love. This time I—"

There was a sudden knock at the door. Brady wheeled around and then hissed, "Who is it, Dilly? Is it your marshal?"

In reply, Dilly threw her head back and did the only thing that came to her mind and that was to scream a warning for Custis.

Brady cursed and jumped forward, smashing her full in the face with his gloved hand. Dilly crashed to the floor unconscious.

"What's going on in there!" the voice in the hallway demanded. "Open up!"

Brady drew his gun and jumped to the door. He would shoot the marshal right where he stood and then he'd shoot Dilly and be gone from this shabby apartment building before anyone could see him, much less foil his escape.

Brady threw the deadbolt and stepped back ready to fire. The door swung open and there stood a young man with a medical bag in his hand.

"Who . . ." The doctor's eyes swept past Brady to Dilly lying unconscious on the floor. "What have you done to her!"

Brady struck the doctor across the back of the head with the barrel of his gun. Hit him hard enough that he might even have killed the man, although he doubted it. Now, he was flying out the door and racing for the street. There was no point in executing Dilly and the young doctor. A respected doctor was highly regarded and valued. Killing this pair would have brought the entire city police department down on Brady in a relentless manhunt.

Brady knew where the marshal and Dilly could be found and he would bide his time in wait for the perfect opportunity to kill them *both*.

Chapter 9

As Longarm approached his apartment building, he saw a crowd gathering while a city policeman was trying hard to keep the entrance to the building open. A horse-drawn ambulance stood waiting at the curb. Longarm knew in an instant that something bad had happened and he hoped it was not in his own apartment. He bolted forward and when the policeman tried to block his path, Longarm said, "Federal officer. Let me pass!"

The policeman stepped aside and Longarm bounded up the stairs to see a doctor and nurse bent over someone lying unconscious on his living room floor. There was another policeman standing by the doorway who Longarm recognized and liked.

"Officer, what happened?" he asked the policeman, eyes darting first to Dr. Wilson, who was being raised onto a stretcher, and then to Dilly.

"This your apartment?" the policeman, whose name Longarm had forgotten, asked.

"Yes."

The officer shook his head. "Someone came here and attacked the young lady and Dr. Wilson. The attacker was seen flying down the stairs and then he disappeared into the street below.

Longarm suddenly remembered the officer's name. It was George Cowan. "Do you have a description, Officer Cowan?"

The policeman nodded. "The attacker was tall with a neatly trimmed black beard and mustache. Well dressed. Late thirties and—"

"That's enough," Longarm said.

Cowan looked closely at Longarm "Do you know who did this?"

Longarm ignored the question because he wanted to catch and take care of Jim Brady all by himself. "How badly are they hurt?"

"The doctor was hit hard. He's in rough shape. The woman looks like she was already hurt and this sure didn't help."

"No," Longarm said, "it didn't."

Officer Cowan shifted on his feet. He was a veteran city policeman and certainly nobody's fool. "Marshal Long, if you know who did this, then you have to tell me his name. We'll scour the town to find and arrest whoever did this to them. You probably know that Dr. Wilson is very popular around here and there are going to be a lot of upset folks. I've never heard a bad word about him. In fact, some people think that the doc is almost a living saint."

"I know that," Longarm said as they got Wilson strapped down on a litter and two men started taking him down to the ambulance. "Where are they taking Dr. Wilson?"

"To Saint Joseph's Hospital. The young woman will go to the other hospital."

"Send her to Saint Joseph's too," Longarm ordered.

"It's expensive. Can she can pay for the better medical?"

"Tell the people at Saint Joseph's that her bill will be taken care of in full."

"All right," the policeman said. "But who the hell did this?"

Rather than reveal Jim Brady's name, Longarm said, "Name slips my mind all of a sudden."

Officer Cowan shook his head. "Marshal Long, you ain't thinkin' of what I think you're thinkin' . . . are you?"

"Nope. Lock up my apartment when you go, Officer."

"I'll do it," the policeman promised. He lowered his voice and caught Longarm by the shoulder as he was about to turn and leave. "Marshal Long, if you need any help from Denver's finest, you say the word and I'll get a few of my friends and we'll take care of whoever did this *unofficially*." The policeman winked. "You know what I mean?"

"Yeah, I know what you mean. But I can handle it."

"Are you sure?"

"Dead sure," Longarm vowed.

"I hope so," the policeman said. "Because whoever did this has no heart or soul. Only an animal would do something like this to a woman and a doctor who never hurt anyone in his life."

"I'll take care of the attacker," Longarm repeated. "And when Miss Dilly wakes up, please tell her I'll be visiting just as soon as I see and take care of Jim."

"Will do."

Longarm headed back down the stairs with his mind racing like a runaway train. Where would Jim Brady run for cover? Certainly not his plush hotel room unless it was only for a few minutes to collect his valuables, money, and perhaps a few extra weapons and any important documents.

Longarm barged through the curious crowd outside in the street. Several of the people who lived in his apartment called out to him with questions, but he ignored them and ran to the corner.

Maybe, just maybe he could still catch Brady emptying his room at the Dakota, or as he was leaving. It was worth a try.

Longarm sprinted down the street, cutting across a vacant lot and hoping that he could find Brady and put a stop to the man once and for all.

Jim Brady knew that he needed to look composed and casual when he entered the Dakota. He waved at the clerk at the registration desk with a smile of unconcern and then sauntered over to the desk and asked if he had any mail.

"No mail today, Mr. Brady."

"That's good. It means no bills." Brady laughed and the registration clerk laughed as well although it seemed somehow forced. Brady said, "I'll be taking a nap and don't wish to be disturbed for the rest of the afternoon."

"Yes, sir." The clerk appeared troubled and acted as if he wanted to say something, but he didn't.

"Anything wrong?" Brady asked.

"Not a thing," the clerk replied.

"Glad to hear it."

Brady strolled up the winding staircase to his room. But once out of sight, he rushed down the hall fumbling for his room keys. He needn't have bothered because his door was unlocked.

Brady froze, thinking, *I never leave my door unlocked.*

A maid appeared pushing a laundry cart down the hallway. She was old and missing several of her front teeth, but she was always cheerful despite her sad circumstances and called, "Afternoon, Mr. Brady!"

"Afternoon, Neddy. Say, have you been in my room to tidy up and replace the towels and sheets already?"

"No, sir. But some other gentleman was in there. I thought he was visiting you this morning."

Brady felt his heart begin to race. "Was he a tall man with a brown hat and coat?"

"That's the one."

"Did you notice if he stayed in the room long?"

"He wasn't in there for long. He left less than an hour ago, Mr. Brady. Didn't say a word to anybody. Just came and left. Was he a good friend of yours?"

"Uh, yeah. An old friend. Thanks, Neddy."

Brady gave the old woman a silver dollar and she smiled happily. "You're a good and generous man, sir!"

"And you do a fine job here, Neddy."

Brady entered his room and locked the door behind him, feeling a panicky sweat break out across his chest and back. The big federal marshal Custis Long had been here earlier snooping around in his hotel room. Marshal Long might even be watching the hotel right now!

Brady sneaked up to his window and eased a corner of the curtain aside. He scanned the street below for several minutes until he was sure that Marshal Long was not spying on him or lying in wait for an ambush. Satisfied, he took a deep breath and set about preparing for his hurried departure.

Brady grabbed two matching leather satchels and began stuffing them with all his money, jewelry, and the extra guns and knives he most prized. He also added a change of underclothing and a starched shirt. Brady hated to think that he would have to abandon his expensive wardrobe and extra shoes, but there was no help for it. Because the federal marshal knew where he was lodging, every minute he remained here at the Dakota increased his chances of getting caught and arrested. They'd pin the baby's death on him and maybe the doctor's death, too, if the man had died. A doctor and a newborn child would get him a quick hangman's noose.

It took Brady less than five minutes to pack the large black leather satchels and he had to struggle to zipper them closed. Hefting them off the bed, he carried them to his door and set them softly on the rug. He slowly turned the bolt and then eased the door open, heart pounding, half expecting Marshal Long to be waiting outside to pounce.

But the hallway was empty.

"Whew!" Brady breathed.

He grabbed up his satchels and set them in the hallway. He locked his door and then picked up the satchels again and started to go downstairs. Suddenly, he halted midstride and changed direction. Brady remembered that there was an old, unused fire exit ladder that he could take down to the back alley. It would allow him to leave without anyone knowing it and also to avoid the big marshal should he come charging up from the lobby.

The fire exit door creaked loudly in protest as he shoved it open on its heavy, rusted hinges. Brady set his satchels down and grabbed the fire ladder, then released it and pushed it downward. The ladder was rickety and appeared as if it had never been unhinged. Brady surveyed the alley below and it was clear. He had to pick up his satchels and place them on the ladder as he swung a leg over a small railing. When he did so, the ladder tipped unexpectedly and both heavy satchels dropped off the ladder and crashed down into the alley.

"Damn!" Brady swore, knowing that there were sometimes derelicts that hid out in the alley and that they would just love to have his cash and other valuables land on them like manna from heaven.

And in fact, *two* derelicts suddenly appeared from the trash and clutter below. Brady could not see their faces because they both were old, floppy hats and the lighting was poor.

The pair did see him, however. They furtively glanced up at Brady on the second-floor landing and saw that he was attempting to descend on the creaky fire ladder.

The pair exchanged a whoop of delight, then ran, each grabbing a satchel.

"Hey!" Brady shouted. "Those are mine. Drop them, damn you!"

There was no way that Brady could get down into the alley fast enough to stop the pair so he did the only thing he could do. He whipped out his revolver, took dead aim, and shot both men in the back before they could round the corner of the alley and disappear. One of the derelicts, however, was only badly wounded. Shot, it appeared, in the buttocks. He was on the ground howling in pain, but now pushing to his feet and grabbing both satchels. He glanced up at Jim Brady screaming curses. Brady took aim and fired a third time, drilling the man, who spun completely around and fell behind some trash cans moaning and gasping as he faced death.

Brady left the man to die and shouted, "That'll teach you thieving sonofabitches!"

With a smile of satisfaction he slammed the ladder down and then began to descend into the alley.

"Help!" the one he shot twice whispered. "Help me, please!"

"Die, you worthless piece of dog shit!"

Brady holstered his gun. The two derelicts would never be missed. As far as Jim Brady was concerned, he'd done Denver a favor by killing them. But the three shots would be heard out in front of the hotel and would draw attention. And that was why he had to get as far away from this place as quickly as was humanly possible.

Chapter 10

Longarm was just about to sprint up the front entrance stairs into the Dakota when he heard three distinct gunshots emanating from the back alley behind the large and impressive hotel. He drew his six-gun and headed around behind the building, remembering the fire escape ladder that dropped down into the back alley. There was no one else he could think of that would be using that escape other than Jim Brady.

But it was a long way around the building and when Longarm finally got to the alley, he saw Brady barreling straight at him. The two men skidded to a halt and Longarm fired first without taking aim. His bullet creased Brady's face and the gambler dove behind some overturned trash cans and returned fire.

Longarm couldn't see anything because his eyes were not yet accustomed to the poor light. But Brady's eyes were completely adjusted and his bullets sent Longarm to the ground where he rolled behind more trash. And then, everything was still. The smell of gun smoke hung in the air, but the stench of rotting rubbish soon filled Longarm's nostrils.

"Brady! Come out with your hands up!" Longarm shouted.

"Go to hell!"

"You can't get out of here alive! You make a run for it and I'll shoot you in the back."

There was a long silence followed by two shots from Brady's pistol and then more silence.

"Brady!" Longarm shouted, wanting to see the man hang. "I won't kill you if you surrender."

"Yeah, but we both know that the city's hangman will. I'd rather take my chances and kill you."

"You got no chance at all," Longarm yelled. "If you think I'm going to shoot you where it won't hurt, you're wrong! I'll *gut* shoot you, Brady. It's what you deserve!"

Brady cursed. "So you're the judge and executioner? That it, Marshal? And have you fucked Dilly a time or two already? I'll bet you have, Marshal. She's pretty good, huh!"

Longarm heard the man's cackling laughter. It confirmed that Jim Brady was crazy. Stark mad, but Longarm knew that a crazed and cornered animal was always the most dangerous.

Then, Longarm heard a ragged howl of pain. And it wasn't coming from Brady.

"Who's that!" Longarm cried.

"A man I shot just before you showed up but didn't kill!" Brady called out. "I've got a knife and I'm going to cut off his damned fingers one at a time if you don't let me go."

"You sonofabitch!" Longarm shouted. "Haven't you got any feelings at all!"

"None whatsoever when it comes to my survival. And I *will* survive. I'm going to cut off his finger right now, Marshal! You're gonna hear him screaming like a stuck hog!"

And Longarm *did* hear a terrible, bloodcurdling scream fill the alley. And then the man began to sob.

Longarm swore and pounded his fist against his chest in helpless frustration. He knew that Brady had a man . . . probably a drunk without any value at all except for the fact that he was a human being in great pain from the torture he was now receiving. Longarm knew that Brady would cut off every one of the drunk's fingers until the derelict bled to death. And Longarm also knew that he couldn't live with that on his conscience.

A bloody stump of finger sailed over the trash cans to land near Longarm. The finger was twitching. Brady yelled, "There's the first one. The little finger. I'm going to saw off his thumb now. It'll probably hurt a whole lot worse, huh, Marshal?"

"Damnit, Brady, leave the poor sonofabitch alone!" Longarm called, feeling an overpowering rage wash over him. "Let's stand up and shoot it out like men!"

"The hell with that, Marshal. I only play the game when the odds are all in my favor."

"What do you want!"

"Throw out your gun and come out with your hands in the air," Brady demanded. "Do that, or in about five seconds I'm going to toss you a bloody thumb!"

Longarm knew that Brady would kill him if he was unarmed. But if he didn't do as he was ordered, Jim Brady was going to slowly torture and then kill an innocent man.

Longarm reached down into his vest pocket and fingered his hidden, double-barreled derringer. He sure hoped it was going to be his ace in the hole as he tossed his six-shot revolver out in the open, then stood up and raised his hands.

"All right, Brady, you can stop torturing that poor bastard and make a run for it."

Brady came out with his gun pointed at Longarm's chest and the distance between them was about fifty feet. Blood trickled out of the gambler's scalp where Longarm's bullet had left its mark. The alley was still now except for the derelict whose gasps and moans were growing faint.

"You're a fool, Marshal. That man is dying. You gave your life for nothing. You drew an empty hand."

"Maybe so," Longarm replied.

"If it hadn't been for you and Dilly . . . Well, the world would have been my oyster. But she got pregnant and you had to go and play the hero. Now, I've lost everything and it's all your fault."

"No, it isn't," Longarm corrected, biding for more time and some answer to take the advantage in this deadly game. "Brady, you'll never agree, but you got exactly what you had coming. Just for the record, did you think you were going to enter Denver's high society? Rub elbows with the rich folks like the Buckinghams? Marry some debutante? Inherit a lot of money?"

"That's about the way I had it figured. I was just waiting to find the right girl. She didn't have to be pretty like Dilly. Dumb and homely would have been just fine so long as her family was rich."

"It would never have worked," Longarm told the man. "You can wrap a pig in silk, but he'll still stink and oink."

Brady cursed under his breath and came a little closer. "You're a dead man talking, Marshal."

Longarm shrugged. "I was born at noon and my old man said I'd die at noon. Said he had a vision that's how it would be. So before you pull that trigger, Brady, I need to know. Is it noon?"

"I don't know or care, Marshal."

"Mind if I check my pocket watch? Oh, and after you kill me, you ought to take my gold watch. It's worth plenty."

Brady laughed and walked closer. He was now well within range of the hidden derringer. "I'll give you this much, Marshal, you've got more than your share of guts. Yeah, let's see that valuable pocket watch. But, if it isn't noon . . . Well, too damned bad because your time is up."

Longarm reached into his vest pocket and drew out his watch and chain. He palmed the derringer and pretended to study the watch while taking a few steps closer to Brady.

"Well," Brady asked, "what time is it?"

Longarm cocked the hammer of the derringer, turned it on the gambler, and fired both barrels in less than a heartbeat. Brady was knocked back half a step. His revolver bucked a bullet into the trash. Then, he swayed and his lips moved in silence as a bloody froth appeared on them.

"I guess my old man was wrong," Longarm said quietly. "It's high noon, but I'm not the one that's dead."

Brady pitched over onto his face. Longarm hurried past the dead gambler and knelt beside the derelict. The man smelled as bad as the garbage he lay behind and he was a goner.

Longarm saw a second derelict lying facedown in the alley. He went over and checked, but this man was also dead. Longarm picked up the two satchels that had cost the pair their lives. He inspected them, finding bundles of cash, jewelry, and weapons.

"Must be a thousand dollars cash plus the value of the rest of Brady's belongings," Longarm said quietly to himself. "Plenty enough to pay for everything that Dilly will need at Saint Joseph's and then maybe some new clothes and a train ticket to somewhere for a fresh start."

Longarm picked up the satchels and headed out of the fetid alley. He would take the satchels up to his apartment and tell no one about them. Everything would go to pay the hospital bills of Dilly and Dr. Wilson . . . and the remainder to a local charity.

"Thanks for being a successful gambler," Longarm said glancing back at Brady's body. "You have my word of honor that your poker winnings will all go to good and worthy causes."

Chapter 11

Longarm was sitting at his office desk two weeks later when Billy Vail came around for a visit. "How are you feeling, Custis?"

"As good as new."

"Glad to hear that, because you're probably headed off to Prescott, Arizona, in the next few days."

Longarm leaned back in his chair and laced his fingers behind his neck. "What happened out there?"

Billy sat down in an chair. "That's the question I'm asking. Deputy Ben Tucker hasn't reported in for over a week. Every morning I look for his telegram, but there's nothing."

"How often was he supposed to send you a telegram?"

"Every other day," Billy said, unfolding a telegram and removing his reading glasses. "Custis, this was the last one that I got from Tucker and it is short and sweet.

Marshal Vail. I finally have a solid lead on who killed Governor-Elect John Benton. I will be renting a horse and outfit and be out of touch for a few days. Hope to capture killer and bring to trial by Friday.

"Today is only Monday, Billy." Longarm shrugged. "You

know how things can take longer than expected when you're tracking a fugitive. Give Ben a little more time."

But Billy shook his head. "Custis, this telegram was sent last Monday. That's an entire week ago from today."

"Maybe Ben had to rent a slow horse," Longarm deadpanned.

"Not funny," Billy groused.

Longarm stopped grinning. "Look. Arizona has a lot of wide open country and a good part of it is remote mountains and hot, empty desert. If I were you, I wouldn't be too concerned for at least another week."

"Custis, if it were *you* out there instead of Ben, I wouldn't be concerned because you don't keep track of time or follow my orders. Ben, however, is a stickler for reporting in and following orders. So when he disappears for a week, I have good reason to be worried."

"You know what," Longarm said, "just about the time you put me on the westbound train for Arizona, Ben Tucker is going to send you a telegram saying that he caught the killer and the man is in jail awaiting sentencing. And by then, I'll be ridin' the rails someplace between here and Arizona and you won't have any way to get ahold of me. It'll all amount to a big waste of my time and the taxpayers' money."

Billy got up and began to pace back and forth. "Of course, you could be right for a change. But I still have a bad feeling in my gut that something has gone haywire in Arizona."

"Maybe the bad feeling in your gut is because you had something awful to eat at lunch that didn't agree with your sensitive stomach," Longarm said with a lopsided grin.

Billy was not in any mood to suffer Longarm's humor. "What are you working on right now?"

"Not much. Just some odds and ends that I'm tying up."

"Well," Billy said, "be sure to tie them all up by tomorrow

and be ready to leave if I give the word. You might also be interested to know that Ben Tucker's wife stopped by my office first thing this morning to ask about her husband."

Longarm's smile faded. "What did you tell Ethel?"

Billy cleared his throat and his shoulders slumped. "She was obviously very concerned so I advised her not to worry and assured her that her husband was just fine."

"Good," Longarm said. "What else could you do?"

"What I said is good if it is the truth," Billy snapped. "But, god forbid, if Ben is in trouble, hurt, or even dead . . . then I'm going to end up cutting my own wrists."

Longarm got up and stared out the window thinking about Ben Tucker, who was his friend and also a very good law officer. "Ben's most likely out somewhere in the desert or mountains where there isn't a telegraph. But if you don't hear from him in the next few days, I'll be on the train."

"Let's just hope that it doesn't come to that," Billy said as he started to go back to his own office. "By the way, I understand that young woman you saved has been released from Saint Joseph's."

"That's right. She and Dr. Wilson are both on the road to a complete recovery."

"Sure glad to hear that," Billy said with relief. "I hear that her real name is Miss Delia Hamilton and she's the daughter of a very wealthy family that lives in Philadelphia."

"That's correct."

"Where is the young woman staying now?"

Longarm had been hoping that Billy wasn't going to ask that very question. "Uh . . . She's staying with . . . with me."

Billy stared at him with strong disapproval written all over his face. Longarm's boss was a very straightlaced and religious man who did not countenance Longarm's many and usually fleeting amorous relationships.

"Relax, Billy. The girl is still recovering and she needs a safe, quiet place to rest for a while."

"Custis, this isn't some common girl you picked up in a rowdy saloon! This is the daughter of a wealthy man and she comes from a very respectable family."

"So I've been told."

"Then let her remain respectable!"

"Billy, are you forgetting that Delia had Jim Brady's baby out of wedlock? And that she was living with that gambler? Now I'm not judging her in the least, but she was no blushing virgin when I saved her life and took her into my humble abode."

Billy snorted. "Perhaps she has made costly moral mistakes. But that doesn't mean that you should compound them. Good heavens, Custis, release the poor woman and see that she is on the next eastbound to her family where she will be protected!"

Longarm decided that he might as well let Billy have it with both barrels. "Actually, I've already tried to get Dilly to leave for Philadelphia and she says she will . . . but only if I go with her."

"What!"

"Miss Delia Hamilton is sure that she's in love with me," Longarm told his boss. "And she wants me to go to Philadelphia to ask her father for her hand in marriage."

Billy had been about to leave the room, but now he came back inside and plopped down again in the office chair. "I don't believe it!"

Longarm shrugged. "Believe it or not, I'm telling you the truth. Dilly—or Delia if you prefer—will not leave my apartment. I saved her, I killed the man who was trying to kill her, and now I'm her knight in shining armor."

"Then I shall have to talk to her and make the poor soul see the true you!"

"I'd rather that you didn't do that," Longarm said. "In fact, I insist that you keep your nose out of our affair."

"Why should I do that if it is not in her best interest?"

"Because I . . . Well, I'm very attached to Dilly."

Billy groaned and leaned way back in the chair, so far that it almost tipped over. Then, he stared at Longarm and said, "You can't be serious!"

"I am serious."

"But . . . But she comes from a wealthy family and you come from . . . well who knows where you came from. You've never been willing to discuss your past."

"You know that I'm from West Virginia, Billy. And not from poverty, either. But that is neither here nor there. The fact of the matter is that I am considering going to Philadelphia and meeting her family."

"No!"

"I'm sorry." Longarm scowled. "Maybe this is the one. Maybe Dilly is the woman I was meant to marry."

Billy threw both hands up in the air and stared at the ceiling in disbelief. "Have you gone insane!"

Longarm drew a cheroot from his pocket. "You know something? I was actually thinking that you might be happy for me if I choose to marry Miss Hamilton. For years you've been badgering me to stop being a rogue and a ladies' man. You've told me over and over about the wonder of marriage and the godliness and virtue of fidelity."

"Sure I have, but I always knew that I was whistling in the wind."

"Well, maybe your words have actually had some effect," Longarm said. "Because I am considering going to Philadelphia to meet Dilly's family and perhaps become a part of it."

"You'd go crazy in the East! What do you think you'd do back there . . . sit in some fancy office and make big

93

financial deals?" Billy scoffed. "Why you can't even budget your money enough to last from one federal paycheck to the next. You're always broke and borrowing money from me."

"That I never fail to pay back!"

"Sure, but you'll never be a man who handles money well. The only things you handle well are guns and women."

Longarm lit his cheroot and blew an angry smoke ring between them. "I can see that you're in a prickly mood today, Billy. Probably caused by the worry over Ben Tucker's lack of communication. Because of that, I forgive your bad manners and think that we've said about enough to each other for one day."

"I couldn't agree more!" Billy shouted. "But if you think you're going to marry that woman and live the life of leisure and luxury in Philadelphia, then you don't know the first thing about yourself."

With those ringing words, Billy stormed out of the office leaving Longarm to puff his cheroot and stare out the window wondering if Billy might be slightly on target with his harsh and outspoken judgment.

Chapter 12

Longarm walked back to his apartment after work with a world of worry on his mind even though, by nature, he was not a worrier. His conversation with Billy Vail had been troubling and had left him wondering if his boss was right about his true nature—that he was not cut out for finances or fidelity.

When he climbed the steps to his apartment, he happened to bump into old Mrs. Harney. She smiled at Longarm and said, "That young woman, Dilly, she's a sweet girl. I showed her how to cook a nice stew for your dinner. She told me that you two are in love and planning to go to Philadelphia to get married."

"Well, ma'am, I don't know about getting married. That's sorta jumpin' the gun, so to speak."

"But she *loves* you, Marshal!" Suddenly, his landlord was getting upset with him. For Longarm, it was about as much as he could abide—Mrs. Harney and Billy both trying to tell him how to live his life. "That's a *nice* girl. Not like most of the ones you bring here. You are gonna marry her, aren't you?"

"I'm not sure."

"Why not!"

It was Mr. Harney who had overheard the conversation and had come out in his bathrobe and slippers to join the argument.

"Look," Longarm said, trying to keep the exasperation out of his voice. "Dilly, I mean Miss Hamilton, is not yet well. It's no secret that she just recently lost her baby. And you've both seen how badly she was beaten."

"Yeah, but you killed that sonofabitch Jim Brady, didn't you?" Mr. Harney demanded. "That's what we read in the newspaper."

"Well, I did kill him," Longarm admitted. "But everything has happened real fast and we need some time to sort of sort things out."

"The girl loves that orange Tiger cat of yours, too," Mrs. Harney said, trying to make Longarm feel even guiltier. "She was down yesterday asking where she could buy the cat some fish. And I told her that sardines would do and then I gave her a couple of cans."

"Tiger will appreciate that very much," Longarm said, wondering if such a fine dinner might ruin Tiger's appetite for alley garbage plus whatever scraps he could get under Longarm's table. "I just don't want him to get spoiled."

"You'd better marry that young lady," Mrs. Harney said accusingly. "She thinks you walk on water."

"Well, I can't," Longarm snapped. "Now, if you'll excuse me."

The couple was blocking the stairs so that he couldn't pass. Longarm had to shoulder the old folks aside and continue up the steps to his apartment.

The door was unlocked and he went right in to find Dilly in the kitchen humming some tune. The young woman's face was healing fast and she was already quite a beauty. Meanwhile, the alley cat, Tiger, was lying stretched out on Longarm's couch licking his lips clean of fresh sardines. Dilly had been brushing him and the cat had never looked so clean and respectable.

"Hi, darling," she called, coming over to kiss him on the lips. "I'm cooking pork chops for supper. And I've made an apple pie for dessert. Your favorite."

"Smells delicious."

"I hope that you're famished," Dilly said with a radiant mile. "Did everything go all right at your office?"

"As a matter of fact," Longarm said, "there is a problem. Do you remember that deputy that my boss sent to Arizona?"

"Yes. You said he was a good man by the name of Ben Tucker."

"That's right. Well, the problem is that he's missing."

"How could you or your boss know that?"

"He was supposed to send telegrams every few days and he hasn't done that for over a week."

"Oh, my," Dilly said, going back to the stove. "Well, I hope the poor man is all right. Maybe he fell ill or off a horse or something."

"Billy says he has a bad feeling that Ben has gotten himself into far more serious trouble."

"That is a shame."

"Dilly, I'm probably going to have to head out to Arizona and find out what happened to Ben."

Now Longarm had her full attention. "But . . . But you can't go now, Custis. I was hoping that we could leave for Philadelphia next week. Remember us talking about it?"

"Sure. And I'd like to go, but I can't turn my back on another law officer that's in trouble."

"Maybe he just quit and decided to do something else for a living. Or the man fell in love, got married, and sailed to the Canary Islands for a honeymoon. Custis, you know that lots of good things could have happened to the man instead of just bad."

"I know that," Longarm agreed. "But the thing is, Ben Tucker loved being a federal law officer and he wouldn't have just quit and left Billy Vail hanging. He'd have resigned formally and sent a telegram to that effect and probably also an official letter. Besides, he's married, and his wife, Ethel, is also very worried."

Dilly's eyes clouded. "I don't want you to leave us, Custis. Tiger and I need you here."

Longarm didn't bother to tell the dear woman that Tiger was perfectly able to make his own way in life and had been doing it for years. But Dilly, well, that was another thing entirely. She was still fragile and afraid.

"Dilly, I promised my boss that, if we didn't hear from Ben in a few days, I'd go to Arizona and find him. He could be in deep trouble and I have to do what I can for the man."

She nodded her head. "Can I come with you?"

"No. You need to rest and . . . and take care of the cat."

"Maybe Ben will send a telegram tomorrow or the next day and then we can still go to Philadelphia together next week for a visit. Your landlord has promised me that she'll look after Tiger."

"We'll see."

"Sit down at the table and I'll pour you a glass of whiskey and then we can eat."

Longarm thought that sounded very domestic and like a good idea. Dilly, he'd discovered, was a surprisingly good cook. She had confessed that her mother had insisted that she take cooking lessons from the chef that they employed.

Later that evening, Longarm and Dilly went to bed and made love. It wasn't wild or passionate love, but it was good and very satisfying. And afterward, Dilly said, "If you have to go to Arizona and I can't come with you, then I'll wait right here with Tiger until you return."

"Okay."

"But I want you to promise me that you'll go to Philadelphia to meet my family after Arizona."

Longarm wasn't quite ready to make that promise. "Dilly, I don't think I'm cut out to be anything but a Western lawman."

"You think that, because you don't know how many opportunities there are in other places. At the very least, you owe us both the chance to explore those opportunities."

"I'll think about it."

"Promise me that you'll at least go to Philadelphia for one week."

"All right," he conceded. "But your family might not like me. They might find me . . . rough."

"They'll love you," Dilly said, hugging him tightly. "And when we move back there, we have to be sure to take Tiger."

"He might not want to go," Longarm told her. "Cats are sorta set in their ways and like to make their own decisions."

But Dilly wasn't convinced. "Sometimes, like big, strong men, they need to be shown better ways and better places."

"Do tell," Longarm said, wondering if he and Tiger were both being gently, but very firmly, pushed in a direction they both did not want to go.

Chapter 13

Longarm left his apartment early the next morning to go to work after kissing Dilly good-bye at the door. He descended his stairs and stepped out into the street, which was already busy with pedestrians and wagons all going to work or about their daily routines.

"Fine day, Marshal!" a tall, clean-shaven young man wearing a dark green coat and derby hat said in a cheerful voice. He smiled broadly and reminded Longarm of someone he had met in the very recent past.

"Indeed it is," Longarm said, taking in a deep lungful of the fresh and invigorating morning air and then starting off to work.

The young stranger fell in beside him. "On your way to the federal building, huh."

"Yep. Another day and another dollar," Longarm replied, thinking that maybe he didn't want to work at his federal job until retirement. Maybe going to Philadelphia would be a life-changing experience.

"I read about you in the paper the other day, Marshal. Sounds like you sure were lucky killing that man."

"Luck had something to do with it," Longarm said, feeling slightly irritated by this man who kept interrupting his thoughts. "But there is always an element of skill involved."

"I'm sure that there was. You've killed quite a few men in your time, I'd guess."

Longarm glanced sideways with irritation. "More than I care to remember," he replied, thinking that he really had seen this face before.

"Yeah, I'll bet you have." The young stranger gave him an odd smile and then they reached the end of the block. "But everyone's luck runs out sooner or later, Marshal."

Longarm thought that was a queer thing to have someone tell him, but before he could formulate a reply, the tall, good-looking young man wearing the derby disappeared into the crowd. Odd thing for a complete stranger to say, Longarm mused, putting the man out of his mind.

Longarm continued strolling down the street enjoying the fine Denver morning and tipping his hat to the ladies he passed, yet he became preoccupied thinking about Dilly and perhaps soon visiting Philadelphia. He had never liked the East, and yet he wanted to find out if there was a new world back there that he ought to at least consider exploring. Dilly—or rather Delia—wanted to introduce him to people and places that might one day make him a rich and successful man. Was that so wrong? And if he didn't go to Philadelphia, would he always wonder if he should have at least looked into what new opportunities might have been his to pursue?

These questions were so compelling to Longarm that he became lost in thought and he didn't realize that the man in the green derby and two other men had fallen in just a few steps ahead of him. But at the end of another block, they held back until Longarm was halfway across the street and then they followed.

"I wonder what Dilly's father is like?" Longarm mused aloud to himself as he approached a small tobacco shop where he liked to buy his daily cigar. He was running a few minutes late for work, but he was out of cigars so he entered the store and made his purchase.

"I've got some new stock from Cuba," the tobacconist told Longarm. "You really ought to try one."

"Maybe tomorrow. How much do they cost?"

"Four bits and worth every penny, Marshal. They are much more pleasurable to smoke than those two-bit Virginia cigars that you buy from me."

"I'm sure they are," Longarm told the merchant. "But if I get hooked on Cubans, I'll be spending too much money each month and have to cut back on something else. So maybe it's better that I stick with what I already like to smoke."

The tobacconist laughed. "I'll let you have one of those Cubans for free since you're such a good and regular customer. Then I'll have you hooked forever on 'em!"

It was their small joke. The tobacco store owner was always trying to introduce Longarm to more expensive cigars and so Longarm just waved him off and continued on toward his office. His mind went right back to Dilly and Philadelphia. He'd never even asked her if she had any brothers or sisters.

Out of the corner of his eye, he saw the same tall man in the green derby approach him with two burly, unsmiling friends. They acted as if they didn't see Longarm, but he had the impression that they were focused on him like he was their prey.

Alarm bells went off in Longarm's head and they really got loud when the tall one jammed a gun into Longarm's side and hissed, "Don't say a word, Marshal. Just pretend that you're going to work—only make a turn into the next alley."

Had there only been this one man in the green derby hat, Longarm might have decided to forcefully refuse what he was sure was an unhealthy invitation. But now there were the two others and Longarm knew that they also had guns aimed at his sides.

"What's this about?" Longarm asked as he slowed and neared the alley. "Do I know you fellas?"

"Call me Dan."

"Well, Dan, I'm a federal marshal and you boys are getting yourselves into very serious trouble."

"Oh, it's not *us* that's in trouble," Dan answered. "You are the one that is going to have to pay the piper. Now shut up and turn into this alley!"

Longarm came to an abrupt stop and planted his feet on the pavement. "Dan, why are you three doing this?"

"Maybe you can figure that one out when I tell you that my last name is Brady."

A chill shot down Longarm's spine. "Look, Dan. I'm sorry, but your brother only got what he deserved."

"And so shall you, Marshal. Now shut up or I'll drop you right here on the street in front of all these people, so help me God!"

Longarm's mind was racing and he didn't see any way to avoid going into the alley with these three men. And once in the alley, he knew he would never come back out alive.

"Hey, Tom! Tom Elliot," he shouted as he saw a coworker whose desk sat not more than ten feet from his own at the federal building. "How are you doing this morning?"

Tom Elliot was a well-liked midlevel administrator. Everyone agreed that he was a nice guy who mainly shuffled papers and worked hard to do a good job. He also loved to get Longarm talking about criminals. Longarm knew the man admired him greatly for the exciting life that he lived tracking down outlaws. Longarm didn't make as much money as Tom Elliot, but his job was sure a lot more exciting than shuffling endless stacks of paperwork.

"Why, hello, Marshal Long," Elliot said, smiling. "How are you doing this beautiful morning?"

"Just fine."

Elliot looked at the three tight-lipped men crowded around Longarm and said, "Gentlemen, I don't think I've had the pleasure of your acquaintanceship."

Longarm now thought that he might have found a way to avoid being forced into the alley. Yet he had to be careful so that his unsuspecting coworker didn't get dragged into this trouble and perhaps shot to death.

Longarm smiled and began introductions. "This handsome young fellow in the green derby is Dan. But these other two . . . Well, I haven't been properly introduced to them, either."

"Pleased to meet you," Tom said, extending his hand.

But all three held guns tight in their fists.

With a puzzled expression, Tom finally glanced down at Dan's fist and saw the pistol pressed to Longarm's side. Tom's smile froze on his lips a moment before he asked in a strained voice, "What's going on here, Marshal?"

"They want me to go with them into this alley," Longarm said, pointing. "But I don't think that would be very good for my health."

Dan turned his weapon on Tom now and hissed, "Okay, buster. You just had to butt in and get yourself invited to this private party, didn't you? So why don't you make a little detour with the rest of us into this alley and we'll sort everything out."

But Longarm shook his head at his coworker, saying, "The only thing you can do is to run for your life, Tom. Do it *now*!"

And Tom did whirl, duck, and run. Dan swore and raised

his pistol to shoot Tom in the back. But Longarm slammed his shoulder into the Irishman, then spun around and kicked out desperately trying to knock the other two men down.

Shots exploded and Longarm's hand streaked across his waist for his own weapon, which he drew and fired in one smooth, well-practiced motion. He shot one of the men in the belly, and then he tripped over something and fell, which probably saved his life. Bullets ricocheted off the sidewalk around him and Longarm rolled and fired twice more. The second man squatted down heavily on his haunches with blood pouring out of his broad chest. He stared stupidly at the bullet holes for an instant, then toppled over face first onto the sidewalk. Longarm swung around looking for Dan Brady, who was now racing up the sidewalk and knocking pedestrians aside in his haste to escape.

To his credit and good sense, Tom Elliot was nowhere to be seen. Longarm was quite certain that his coworker was sprinting to the federal building to get help from the marshals.

Longarm started after Dan Brady, sure that the Irishman would try to ambush him sometime in the future in order to exact revenge for the death of his brother. And the last thing that Longarm wanted was a man who would have no qualms about shooting him in the back and maybe even shooting innocent people.

Longarm had always been swift. Being tall he could really cover the distance with his long legs and had been a champion runner when a boy. But now he was older and not in such good shape as he'd been in his youth. And Dan Brady was younger and just as tall. The only good thing was that Brady's dark green derby hat was distinctive and Longarm could see it bobbing over most heads.

Longarm saw Brady disappear around the corner of an old brick building that had once been a firehouse. When he came to that corner, Longarm skidded to a halt, and then took a few gulps of fresh air because his lungs were already burning. He eased around the corner half expecting to find Dan with his gun up and ready to shoot.

But Dan Brady was gone.

Chapter 14

Longarm frantically looked around in all directions without seeing Dan Brady. So he took off running toward Cherry Creek on the hope that Dan had chosen that particular avenue of escape. There was a large city park up ahead and it would be the perfect setting for Dan to wait in ambush, but there were also many ways that he could choose to run back into the city where he could hide from Longarm and the Denver City Police.

Because the weather was so fair, the paths that meandered through the park were being enjoyed by many people this morning, although most of them were older. Some fed the ducks and others were out for the fresh air and exercise. A few were obviously grandparents watching their grandchildren laugh and play. The setting was so peaceful that it was hard for Longarm to accept that somewhere close and perhaps waiting in ambush was a man with a gun in his hand and murder in his heart.

Not wanting to alarm the people enjoying the park, Longarm slipped his Colt revolver back into its holster and composed himself. When an elderly couple slowly walked past, he tipped his hat to them and said pleasantly, "Good morning."

"Good morning!" they called in return.

"Did you happen to see a man running through here just a few moments ago? He was tall and wearing a dark green derby."

"Oh, yes." said the woman sweetly. "He looked to be quite out of breath. I tried to stop him and tell him it was healthier for him to walk vigorously, rather than to run so hard for exercise and perhaps injure his heart. Unfortunately, he didn't even slow down to listen."

"In his case, it really would be healthier to run, ma'am," Longarm said, casting his eyes about. "Which way did he go?"

She turned and daintily raised a silk-gloved hand. "That way," she pointed. "Down along that lovely little path beside the water."

"Thank you."

Longarm had regained his breath and so he took off at a lope that covered ground quickly, but without winding him too fast. When he arrived at the path that followed Cherry Creek, he stopped and looked in both directions. He thought he caught a glimpse of Brady moving through the thick cottonwood trees about two hundred yards away. Longarm set off after the man, passing several more leisurely strollers. He almost collided with a child who emerged laughing from the bushes chasing a duck. He kept running and heard a woman shout angrily in his wake.

It had been a while since Longarm had enjoyed this path along the creek, the last time being with a young lady on a warm day in July. But he recalled that up ahead a few hundred yards the path forked. One fork led to a quaint little wooden bridge that spanned the creek; the other bent back east toward the city. It would be important to be close enough to see which fork Dan Brady took at that junction.

Longarm was gaining ground. He saw Brady run headlong into a gentleman on the bridge and nearly knock him sprawling into the water. He heard the victim's shout of outrage and then Brady was crossing the bridge and heading toward Denver's biggest stockyard where cattle, hogs, and sheep were shipped daily to eastern packing houses.

Longarm went pounding over the bridge and he saw Brady turn to glance over his shoulder. When the man saw Longarm, he found a renewed burst of speed and then hopped a six-foot-high fence and entered the stockyard, which was filled with dust and the sound of restless livestock. Longarm had never been inside the stockyard, but when the wind blew right, you sure could smell it across the city. The stockyard was a maze of pens and alleyways that covered at least twenty acres.

Panting hard now, Longarm came to the perimeter fence and paused, leaning over with both hands on the upper rail while catching his breath. Then he raised his head and scanned the pens, but he couldn't see Dan Brady. The corral on the other side of the fence was filled with milling Longhorn cattle, and Longarm knew that they could be dangerous to a man on foot. Still, if Dan Brady had run the risk of the Longhorns, then he was going to do the same.

Longarm climbed the fence and unfortunately landed with both feet in a big pile of fresh cow shit. He cussed and shook each gooey foot trying to rid himself of as much of the cow shit as possible. But his boots were green to the ankle and the stench filled his nostrils.

Which way now? Brady was no longer in this pen, but which pen had he gone to next?

Longarm was trying to decide when a big brindle bull decided it didn't like humans in his pen and charged, horns down and spanning a good five feet across. For perhaps a split second Longarm thought of drawing his gun and trying to drop the charging beast, but chose the less manly, more intelligent means of survival by leaping to the fence and scrambling to its top rail just as the enraged bull slammed into the rails below.

"Why didn't you do that to Brady!" Longarm yelled at the bull.

Just then a bullet struck his hat and sent it spinning. The bull, a creature of vicious instincts, attacked the hat and soon had it impaled on its horn. Tossing its massive head and stomping, the bull slammed horn and hat into the rail again and again. The hat dropped and the bull stomped it into the dirt and manure.

Longarm, however, hardly noticed because he could see Dan Brady taking aim for a second shot. Heedless of the now excited and milling Longhorns corralled below, Longarm jumped back in the pen with the brindle bull again taking him in its narrow sights.

The corral was about a hundred feet wide and had it been another ten feet, the bull would have run Longarm down and gored him to death. It would have been the most ignoble death imaginable. However, Longarm just made it across and onto the far fence before the brindle hit the nearest post with the force of a miniature locomotive. The post cracked and the entire span of fence sagged precariously. Longarm leapt as another bullet whip-cracked past him and then he sprinted zigzagging through a crowded pen of bawling sheep toward Dan Brady.

The Irishman took aim and fired, but he was out of bullets. He jumped over a fence, causing Longarm to curse at the man's youth and athleticism. Why couldn't Dan Brady have been older, slower, or fatter?

"Stop or I'll shoot!" Longarm bellowed in warning

But Dan Brady wasn't about to stop. He was out of the sheep pen, sprinting through another pen of cattle and then racing down a sloppy alleyway. A mounted cowboy whirling a lariat came galloping down the alleyway shouting something unintelligible at Brady. But when the Irishman raised his empty gun, the stockyard cowboy wheeled his horse around and raced away.

Longarm fired a shot at Brady and saw him stagger, then lurch through the alleyway. Brady struggled over another fence, this one lower, and into a pen of perhaps a thousand huge boars.

"No!" Brady screamed, as they raised their dirty snouts, smelling blood and starting toward him.

Longarm was completely winded when he reached the hog pen. He looked over the low fence and the sight before him was something that would sear his mind forever.

Young, handsome, but badly wounded Dan Brady had fallen in the slop and the hogs were furiously attacking the bleeding man. They were all over Brady, biting and tearing at his flesh. Over their loud and excited snorting and squealing, Longarm heard Brady's insane screams for help, but there was nothing to be done. In the state of mind that all those hogs were in now, Longarm knew it would be suicidal to enter their pen and try to drag what was left of the Irishman away.

"Dear God," Longarm whispered over and over as he watched the hogs eat Dan Brady alive.

The cowboy with the lariat came racing up on his horse and started to yell something to Longarm, but then he saw the hog's feeding frenzy and his jaw dropped.

"It's a man!" the cowboy cried a moment before he leaned far out in his saddle and began to retch.

Longarm bowed his head and then he turned and walked away, not sure where he was going in the great maze of the stockyard pens and alleyways. He only knew that no man deserved to be eaten by a pen of bloodthirsty hogs. And he knew that it would be many a day before he could stomach the sight of pork on his plate.

Longarm was still in a mild state of disbelief when he stumbled back down into Cherry Creek and sat in the clear, cold water. He splashed his face, then began to wash the coating of stinking cow, sheep, and pig shit from his boots and pants. But it wouldn't all come off so he pulled the boots off and threw them in the creek along with his stockings. They sank and he stood up barefooted and then walked over to a trash can where he tossed his shit-splattered coat. He would have done the same with his pants except there were women and children about and he didn't want to offend them with his nakedness.

People stared at Longarm as he trudged down the path toward the city and his apartment. When he arrived, he knocked on the door and Dilly opened it to stare at him in disbelief.

"What—."

Before she could continue, Longarm warned, "You don't want to know what happened."

"But you were just going to work," she said, taking him inside and locking the door. "Darling, you *really* stink!"

"Worse than Tiger ever did," Longarm said, beginning to undress. "Dilly, will you go down the hallway and get the bath filled with very hot water? Make sure there's plenty of soap."

"I will, but—."

"Later," Longarm mumbled. "After I've had a bath and a couple of stiff jolts of whiskey, maybe I'll tell you how my morning went."

She looked closely at him. "Maybe I don't want to know."

"That would be best," he agreed. "Now go draw me a bath and find the whiskey while I undress."

Hours later, Longarm felt like he was half human again and that his mind would eventually recover from the recollection of Dan Brady being devoured by the crazed stockyard boars.

"I want to know," Dilly said, her arm around his broad shoulders. "I want you to tell me what happened."

"First I shot and killed two men about a block and a half from here," Longarm said, explaining what had happened and then how Dan Brady had escaped through the park and into the Denver stockyards.

Dilly was upset. "I knew Dan. He was a lot nicer than Jim."

"Not as nice as you might think."

"Is he . . . Is he dead now?"

Longarm nodded his head. "He is dead and gone. I . . . I really would rather not tell you how he died."

She was paler now and said, "I think I'd rather not know. I'm just so glad that they didn't kill you and—."

There was a loud pounding at Longarm's door. He reached for his revolver and shouted, "Who is it!"

"Billy Vail. Open up, Custis."

Longarm pulled a robe around him. He still smelled of cow and hog shit even though he'd scrubbed himself with a vengeance until his skin was an angry red. "Dilly, please let him in."

She unlocked the door and Billy came barging inside. "What happened! Tom Elliot burst into my office yelling about how three men were going to kill you. We found the two that you shot to death down on the sidewalk, but—."

"The third was Dan Brady and he's also dead," Longarm finished.

"Where?"

Longarm lowered his head with a sad shake.

"Where!" Billy repeated. "We *need* the body."

Longarm raised his chin and looked Billy in the eye. "If you need the body, you're gonna have to start butchering a whole pen of big, hungry boar hogs."

Billy blinked and then swallowed hard. "Are you telling me that . . ."

"Yeah," Longarm said quietly. "They ate him alive."

Dilly's hand flew to her mouth and she ran down the hallway. Longarm could hear her vomiting violently in the bathroom.

"Oh my god," Billy breathed. "It's too horrible to believe."

"Believe it," Longarm told the man. Then he added, "Tomorrow, maybe if Dilly is strong enough, I think I'll board the westbound and go looking for Ben Tucker in Arizona."

"Okay," Billy said, looking lost and distracted as he tried to shake off the nightmarish sight that Longarm had witnessed in the stockyards. "Maybe that would be a damned fine idea. You want me to check in on Dilly and Tiger once in a while?"

"I'd appreciate that," Longarm replied. "Yesterday we went and saw Dr. Wilson at Saint Joseph's Hospital and he's well on the road to recovery. You know, he was engaged to be married to Miss Buckingham . . . but after he got hurt and it looked like he might not fully recover, she broke the engagement."

"She dropped the doctor because he was hurt?"

Longarm nodded. "They thought he might have permanent brain damage and wouldn't fully recover. So Miss Buckingham just told him she was sorry, but she had changed her mind about their getting married."

"That's pretty hard," Billy said.

"Yeah," Longarm agreed. "I don't know which hurt Dr. Wilson the worst—being pistol-whipped so badly, or Miss Buckingham breaking off the engagement."

"If the girl would drop him that easily, he's better off without her," Billy said, with obvious disgust.

Longarm agreed and then he blurted out something he'd not planned on talking about to anyone. "You know something? I think that Dr. Wilson and Dilly are . . . well, kinda right for each other. I think there's a strong attraction between 'em."

"What gives you that impression?" Billy asked.

"I don't know." Longarm shrugged. "I just have that feeling. I can tell things about how women feel."

"Well, Custis, you're the expert on women. As for Dilly and Wilson, I have to admit that they would make a fine match. Don't take this as an insult, but the good doctor would be a better match for Dilly than a big, rough sonof-abitch like you."

"You're probably right about that. One thing I am sure of is that Dilly's rich Philadelphia parents would sure like Dr. Wilson better'n me."

Billy patted Longarm on the shoulder. "Well, don't let it bother you or think too much about it while you're in Arizona. If Dilly is going to fall in love with Dr. Wilson during your absence, you sure won't have any trouble finding your own class of women."

Longarm wasn't sure what Billy meant by that, but he reckoned it meant that Longarm's usual class of women were a little more . . . common than some rich girl from Philadelphia.

"Custis," Billy said, trying to cheer his friend up, "going to Arizona will be a good test of how well Dilly and you are matched in your interests and temperaments. So let it play out and see if you can find and bring back Marshal Ben Tucker alive."

"I'll do that."

There was a long silence between them and then Longarm said in a quiet voice, "I'm glad that no one else besides me had to watch those hogs eat Dan Brady alive. It wasn't something I'll soon forget."

Billy swallowed hard. "I almost get sick just thinking about it."

"Billy, could you use a stiff drink?"

Billy consulted his pocket watch. "It's not even noon, but I believe I could."

"It'll help us both," Longarm assured his boss. "Not much, but some."

Billy nodded with understanding while Longarm padded over to the kitchen to fetch them the bottle and clean glasses.

Chapter 15

Longarm said good-bye to Dilly the next afternoon before he went to the train station and when she kissed him farewell, she said, "Custis, you hurry back and don't worry about Tiger. I'll take good care of him."

"I'm not worried about that big, orange alley cat. Tiger is a survivor like me," Custis told her. "Besides, if you pamper him, he might lose the best part of himself."

Dilly cocked her head a little sideways with a look of confusion. "Sometimes you say the strangest things. Things that make no sense to me at all."

"Does Dr. Wilson ever say strange things that you don't understand?"

"No, but why do you ask?"

Longarm kissed her and hopped on the train as it was pulling out of the station. "Just curious. And you might want to think about that some yourself. Good-bye, Dilly."

"Good-bye and Godspeed, Custis!"

Longarm found a seat on the train and watched Dilly fade into the distance. He knew right down deep in his gut that he'd probably never see Dilly again, or rather Miss Delia Hamilton of Philadelphia's high society. But that was all right so long as he found Ben Tucker and came home alive to his rough old alley cat.

Longarm arrived in Prescott six days later a little worn from his hard travel by train and stagecoach. When he stepped down from the stagecoach, he admired the territorial capitol's fine plaza and offices of government. Not far away was Fort Whipple, which had once protected this part of the territory from Indian attacks, but was now used mostly as an administration and supply center and the Indians were on reservations in this part of north-central Arizona.

Prescott was a beautiful town and its elevation lifted it out of Arizona's searing lower desert so that even in summer the nights were cool and pleasant. Longarm had not been here for more than two years, but he could see that Whiskey Row was still popular among the local cowboys, merchants, and army soldiers.

"Is the town marshal's office still located a block north of here on Cortez Street?" he asked a fella who was standing on the corner reading the local newspaper.

"Sure is and you must be from out of town."

"Denver."

"That country is too cold for me. By any chance are you looking for a good buy on some of our local real estate, mister?"

"Nope."

"Too bad," the man said, looking pained. "The future of this town is unlimited. Soon, there will be a thousand people living here and whatever real estate is bought now will be worth twice as much as it is today. A man with money and good business sense can make a fortune in Prescott."

"Then why don't you just do that?" Longarm replied.

"Oh, I've got the good business sense," the man told him with a sad smile. "Just no funds at this time."

"Then maybe you ought to go to work instead of hanging around in the middle of the day reading the newspaper."

The man folded his paper and eyed Longarm critically from boots to hat, trying to decide if he should offer some smart reply. Apparently, he decided not to take the chance of getting his face rearranged so he simply slapped the paper against his thigh with irritation and walked away.

Longarm found the marshal's office and went inside to see a very heavyset man with a handlebar mustache whose tips were waxed. The lawman's vest was stained by food and grease and he badly needed a shave and haircut. His feet were resting on his desk and it took Longarm a moment to realize that the town officer was sound asleep.

Longarm frowned. He had been hoping that Marshal Gabe Corwin would still be behind that desk. He didn't know this new man, but from his slovenly appearance Longarm could determine that he wasn't half the town officer that Corwin used to be.

"Uh-hem," Longarm coughed.

The fat man started, then instantly went back to sleep. Longarm had just finished a very long journey and he wasn't in a charitable mood so he went over and swept the man's scuffed boots off the desk.

"Hey!" the marshal shouted, now coming awake and jumping to his feet. "What the hell did you do that for? You want to go to jail!"

Without a word, Longarm showed the man his federal marshal's badge.

"Ain't no call for being an asshole," the fat marshal said, sitting down heavily. "So what the hell do you want?"

"What's your name?" Longarm demanded, not even bothering to hide his contempt.

"Clyde. Marshal Clyde Potts."

"Well, Potts, you look like you ought to be run out of

town instead of charged with protecting it. How did someone like you ever take Gabe Corwin's place as town marshal?"

Potts pretended to act offended, but it was a poor show. Instead, he blustered, "I ain't the marshal . . . not quite yet. I'm *acting* marshal, though. Just got to get the town council to approve and pay me."

Longarm hooked his thumbs in his holster belt. "And why on earth would they approve some sorry bastard like you?"

Potts jumped to his feet and Longarm shoved him back down in his chair so hard that he almost spilled over backward. Then Longarm reached down and grabbed Potts by the throat and growled, "Where's Gabe Corwin and where is Deputy United States Marshal Ben Tucker?"

Potts gagged and his face turned red so Longarm released his grip and stepped back. "You even smell worse than you look," Longarm said with contempt. "Don't you ever take a bath?"

"I ain't got time!"

"Oh? But you got the time to sleep at your desk?"

"Listen, Marshal, I got troubles enough without another fed coming into my jurisdiction and giving me a load of grief."

"You don't know the meaning of grief, Potts. And I'm not gonna ask you again where I can find Marshal Corwin and my friend from Denver, Marshal Tucker."

"Old Gabe is dead! If you don't believe me, then go over to the cemetery and look for yourself."

"Marshal Corwin is dead?"

"That's right." Potts dipped his head up and down so that his jowls jiggled. "Marshal Corwin was ambushed with a rifle. He was shot in the back. I've been working night and day trying to find a suspect, but there were no witnesses and no evidence or clues."

"Shit," Longarm swore softly to himself because Corwin had been an outstanding town marshal. "When did it happen?"

"About two weeks ago out behind the livery late one night."

"What would Gabe Corwin have been doing out behind the livery at night?" Longarm demanded.

"No one knows!" Potts had a high-pitched, whiny voice that seriously irritated Longarm as he continued his sorry explanation. "Maybe someone lured old Gabe out there. Or maybe he heard a fight or some drunk raisin' hell behind the barn. No one knows, I tell you."

Longarm saw a chair and wearily took a seat. "Tell me everything you know about Corwin's death, but first tell me about my friend Ben Tucker."

"Tucker came here and made a big show of his authority over us locals," Potts declared with a little smirk. "He asked a lot of questions, none of which he got answers to. He was trying to find out who shot Governor-Elect Benton. But he didn't learn a thing. No more than any of us did."

"So where is Ben Tucker right now?"

Potts shook his head, looking almost pleased. "He just up and disappeared. I think maybe he gave up. I figured he went back to Denver."

"Well, he damn sure didn't," Longarm snapped. "He sent us a telegram saying he was leaving Prescott on the trail of a killer and we haven't heard from him since."

"How was I to know that?" Potts whined. "He sure didn't confide anything to me. As far as I was concerned, Tucker was just wasting everyone's time and he wasn't making any friends in Prescott."

"When was the last time you saw him?"

"About two weeks ago." Potts frowned in concentration. "Actually, it was the same day that old Gabe—I mean

123

Marshal Corwin—was shot in the back. You think there's a connection?"

Potts was smirking again and it was all that Longarm could do not to backhand the fat bastard right out of his chair and onto the floor. Longarm bent over the man and said, "If you're even hinting that Ben Tucker had something to do with Gabe Corwin's death, then I'm going to kick your ass until it's small and bloody enough to slide between those jail bars. Is that understood?"

Potts licked his suddenly dry lips and nodded emphatically. "I sure didn't mean to say that your friend had anything to do with old Gabe's death. Honest, I didn't!"

Longarm folded his arms across his chest. "Then just what *do* you think—if you think at all?"

"I . . . I think that someone killed them both."

Longarm expelled a deep breath. "That's brilliant. But you've no idea who stood to gain by their deaths so that we at least have somewhere to start this murder investigation."

"No, sir. Not yet, but I'm working on it."

This man was simply beyond being pathetic. Longarm reached down and hauled him out of Gabe's office chair and shoved him toward the front door. "Go back to whatever hole you crawled out of, Potts, and don't come back."

"But I'm acting town marshal!"

"Yeah, but I'm acting federal marshal and I say you are out the door right now. You're obviously a sorry sack of shit and I won't have you botching up my investigation."

Half in and half out the door, Potts got a moment of passing courage and yelled, "The town council will see about this! You've gone way beyond your authority in our town. You feds are far too high and mighty, by gawd!"

Longarm made a threatening move toward the door and Potts disappeared. Longarm slammed the door and went over to Gabe Corwin's desk. He wiped it clean of the mud from Potts's boots and sat down in the chair. Then, still fuming and now very frustrated about the death of Corwin and the continued disappearance of Ben Tucker, he closed his eyes and tried to think.

Who, Longarm asked himself, would want to see Marshal Corwin and Ben Tucker dead or out of commission? And who would most benefit from the death of Governor-Elect Benton?

Longarm didn't have a clue, but he was sure that it was all somehow connected just as sure as he was going to find some answers and make some arrests or spill some guilty blood before he left Prescott.

Chapter 16

Early that evening Longarm found the keys to the marshal's office and locked it up tight. There was a cot in the office that he could have slept on, but he had smelled it and knew that Potts had been using that for his bed so he tossed the blankets out back and elected to go to an old two-story brick hotel called the St. Michael just up the street and across from Courthouse Square. There was a nice restaurant on the ground floor of St. Michael and Longarm remembered that it also had a telegraph office. Making a mental note, he tried to remind himself that he needed to send an immediate telegram to Billy Vail that he'd completed the long trip from Denver.

"I'd like to send a telegram to Denver," he told the operator the moment he entered the hotel's lobby.

"Write it out," the little man said with a smile. "Cost you five cents a word."

Longarm scowled. "Kinda steep, isn't it?"

The telegraph operator shrugged his narrow shoulders. "I have to feed my family."

So Longarm simply wrote: *Billy. I've arrived no answers yet.*

The telegraph operator looked disappointed. "Is that it?"

"That's it for today."

"I can't feed my family by sending thirty-cent telegrams."

"Sorry," Longarm said without much sympathy. "I hope to have a lot more to send in a few days."

The telegraph operator took the address and said, "So you must be another federal marshal, huh?"

"That's right."

"I sent a few to Denver for the federal officer named Ben Tucker. He seemed like a nice man, but he acted as if he were pretty frustrated trying to find out what happened to Marshal Corwin and the man that was to be our next governor."

"Yeah," Longarm said, wondering if this little telegraph operator might know something that would help him out. "Marshal Ben Tucker is a fine officer. Did he tell you anything that might help me to understand where he went or why?"

"As a matter of fact, he did say that he was going to follow a lead and ride over to Skull Valley."

"Where is that?"

"The town is over a little mountain range and about fifty miles to the southwest. Pretty little ranching community, or so I'm told."

"Any idea why Tucker would want to go there?"

"I'm afraid not, Marshal. All he said was that it was a lead."

"Anyone important live around Skull Valley?"

"As a matter of fact there are some pretty wealthy ranchers over there. Used to be some outlaws that hung out in those parts, too, or maybe it was Wickenburg. I forget."

"What about Benton?"

"He was shot in the back with a shotgun. Blew a hole out the front of him the size of a watermelon." The telegraph operator clucked his tongue. "The blast splattered that poor man's heart all over the barn wall."

"Was it the same barn that Marshal Gabe Corwin got ambushed behind?"

"As a matter of fact it was."

Longarm thought about this coincidence for a moment and then asked, "What was the governor elect doing behind a barn?"

"Dunno. Dunno why old Gabe was back there either."

"Maybe I better take a look."

"Doubt you'll find anything." The little man brightened. "But you can still see the stains all over that barn wall and little pieces of . . . Oh, well, never mind."

"I doubt it will tell me anything," Longarm said, "but I don't know where else to start looking for evidence."

Longarm started to walk into the hotel lobby, but he turned and said, "Does a girl named Sally still work here serving food and drinks?"

"Sally Mercado?"

"That's the one," Longarm said.

"She ain't a bit Mexican," the telegraph operator said. "Musta married one sometime. Ought to change her name, though."

"Actually, she's half Mexican and half white, but I'll tell her what you suggested," Longarm said dryly.

"I'd rather you didn't," the man said, suddenly looking nervous. "Sally isn't one that likes to be told much of anything."

"I know that," Longarm said. "So I'll do you a favor and forget your advice about her last name."

The little man looked very relieved and nodded his thanks.

Longarm went into the lobby and registered for a room on the second floor. He always preferred being off the ground floor because he liked to be able to survey the street from above with a better view. Also, it gave him a little more time to prepare if he saw trouble coming his way.

Longarm got his room and laid out his belongings. He never slept well on trains or stagecoaches so a nap was in order. Taking off his hat, coat, and boots, he stretched out on the bed and fell asleep almost instantly.

He awoke several hours later and looked out the window to see that it was almost dusk. Longarm stretched and then went down the hall and took a bath. He shaved, combed his hair, and dressed in the last of his clean clothes. The dirty ones he put in a wicker basket just outside his door. A Chinese laundryman prowled the hallways of hotels picking up laundry every few hours. Longarm would have his rumpled suit and shirts washed and pressed and ready by morning.

Longarm checked his six-gun and the derringer to make sure they were in perfect working order. He headed down the stairs hearing the sound of piano music in the hotel bar and his stomach grumbling from lack of decent food.

Longarm went into the saloon first and when he stepped up to the bar, he ordered whiskey and a cigar. The bartender poured and Longarm struck a match to light his cigar, asking, "Is Sally Mercado going to be around this evening?"

"I expect she will be. Most always is."

"Then she didn't get married or—"

"Naw, Sally is much too wild to settle down with one man."

"My kind of woman," Longarm said with a smile.

"Sally is quite a looker and that's for certain," the bartender said. "When I first came to work here, I had a constant big boner and dreamed about getting between her pretty legs."

"So did you?"

"Naw, she never gave me a tumble. Not even when I offered her fifty dollars."

The bartender looked hurt so Longarm tried to console the man by saying, "Sally is hard to figure. I wouldn't take it too hard."

"Oh, I know that. I've seen her go off with men that I knew didn't have a silver dollar to their names. And I've also seen her snub wealthy men who probably would have paid her a king's ransom for her bedroom favors. So you're right about Sally being hard to figure. But I sure wish that she would take a shine to me. My gawd, if I could get her in bed, I'd—"

"Never mind what you'd do," Longarm said, really not wanting to hear any more. "Is she still part owner of this hotel?"

"More than part," the bartender said. "She owns it outright."

"How'd she do that?"

"Poker game. If you didn't know already, Sally is one of the best to ever shuffle a marked deck." The bartender leaned closer and whispered, "But for gosh sake don't tell her I said that."

"I won't," Longarm replied with a smile. "I learned a few years back that it wasn't a good idea to play poker with Sally."

"Some never learn," the bartender told him. "And some are willing to lose a bit just because they like to peek down the front of Sally's low-cut dresses."

"Yeah," Longarm said, "I expect that's true. Sally has a pair of real big ones."

"Like ripe, golden cantaloupes."

"Is the food still good here?"

"Best in town."

Longarm went into the restaurant and it was busy with

prosperous and well-dressed customers. He stood waiting to be shown to a table, but Sally Mercado slipped her arm through his and said, "Right this way, handsome!"

All eyes turned to Longarm as he was escorted by the owner of the hotel, who also happened to be the most beautiful and mysterious woman in Prescott. Tonight Sally was wearing a red silk dress that accentuated every curve of her very curvaceous body. She had long, shiny black hair that she liked to drape over one bare shoulder and a string of gleaming pearls around her neck. Her eyes were dark brown, like agates, and she possessed high cheekbones and full, sensuous lips. When Sally moved across a room it was with the grace of a puma, and men openly stared. Sally didn't mind that; in fact, she loved the attention.

"So, you come to see me after so long, huh?" Sally whispered as a waiter gave them the best table near the fireplace.

"That's right," Longarm said. "How have you been?"

"More than good," she said, studying his face. "Very good." Sally swept her arm out at the roomful of diners. "As you can see, we're doing an excellent business."

"Did you just happen to accidentally intercept me a moment ago?"

Her eyes sparkled with amusement. "No. I don't believe in accidents. And I always check the hotel register to see what surprises await. When I saw your name, Custis Long, my poor heart skipped a beat and there was a place between my legs that began to itch with wet anticipation."

Longarm felt his cheeks warm as Sally sat down close beside him. Under the white linen tablecloth her leg brushed his leg in a way that left little need for rational conversation.

"So, have you come so far to see me . . . or to find out what happened to Ben Tucker?"

"Both," he said, feeling a rise in his pants as her hand

132

slid down to stroke his masculinity. "And I'm here now because I'm hungry."

"Hungry for food—or Sally Mercado?"

He chose honesty. "Both."

She snapped her fingers and a bottle of French wine appeared on ice. The waiter opened the bottle with flair, poured Longarm a taste, and then waited respectfully until he had sipped and sniffed the wine.

"Very good," he said, his voice surprisingly hoarse with growing passion as Sally kept stroking him under the table-cloth.

"Would you like to order now, sir?"

"Steak and whatever else sounds good to your chef."

"Excellent," the waiter said again, bowing slightly before hurrying off to the kitchen.

"Sally," Longarm said as his arousal heightened, "if you don't stop that right now I might lose control and rape you on top of this table."

She giggled. "Custis, you wouldn't have to rape me and it might be fun to do it on the table. But I'm afraid that some of my dinner guests might not find the show to their liking."

"Too bad," Longarm said, removing her hand and pouring her a glass of the expensive wine.

"Business before pleasure tonight, Marshal? Is that how it will be?" she asked, looking a little disappointed.

"Food, drink, and a few questions." Longarm chose his next words with care. "Sally, you must understand that Marshal Ben Tucker is a fine man. He's a friend, husband, and father. I have to find out what happened to him as soon as possible. Can you tell me anything?"

Sally lowered her voice. "This is not the time or the place to talk about these things. I can tell you that I also know your friend and he is a gentleman. A good man. But I do not think you will find him. I think he is dead."

Longarm had been afraid of hearing her confirm his suspicions. "Yes," he said. "Ben would have found a way to get in touch with us in Denver if he were still alive. So what do you think happened to him—and to Governor Benton and Marshal Corwin? So many dead men. There has to be a connection."

Her sensuous lips were almost always curved in a smile, but now they were not. "I do not know who has the answers to these mysteries. But maybe later we can talk and come up with someplace for you to start looking for answers. First, we eat, drink, and then . . ."

She winked, leaving no doubt in Longarm's mind that she expected to be pleasured before she was questioned further.

Longarm raised his glass. "To us, Miss Mercado."

"Yes, to us, my dear, handsome Custis."

"And I understand that you have become sole owner of the St. Michael. Congratulations to you."

"I'm living well and having fun. I make a little love, play a little poker, drink a little wine, and laugh often. What could be more worthwhile in this life?"

They drank and he smiled. "You know, as grim as the situation is here in Prescott and as pessimistic as I am that I will find Ben Tucker alive, just sitting here with you now makes me happy despite all the other problems."

"And me, too." She drank and her free hand again returned to caress his thigh. "And we will get even happier when we go upstairs to my room after you eat. Do you believe that?"

"I believe that," he said with complete sincerity.

Chapter 17

Longarm finished his steak dinner and Sally helped him finish his wine. When Longarm reached for his money, Sally stilled his hand and whispered, "Don't you know that your payment will be made upstairs in my bed?"

"A payment in full," he said, grinning wickedly.

There was a titter as Longarm and Sally Mercado left the dining room and went up the stairs together. Everyone knew what was going to happen and every man in the dining room would have given his front teeth to take Longarm's special place.

Sally's room was really a double suite with a sitting room, small bar, and parlor plus a large and elegantly furnished bedroom with a big four-poster bed and white silk canopy.

"Even nicer than I remembered," Longarm said, slipping off his hat, coat, and gun belt and then taking Sally into his arms. "I'm sure the rest is better than I remembered as well."

Sally embraced him and they kissed passionately. Then she slowly began to finish undressing Longarm, kissing every part of him that was newly exposed. He stood still and shivered with pleasure until Sally had him completely undressed and was cupping his balls in her hands as if they were jewels beyond price or compare.

Her eyes glistened with pleasure as she gazed down on his stiffening manhood and she licked her red lips in anticipation. Then she knelt down and took him into her mouth.

"Mmmmm," she moaned. "About the size and taste of a giant dill pickle."

Longarm threw his head back and laughed. "I've had it described in a lot of ways, but never as a giant dill."

She licked and sucked again and said, "Maybe it's a little sweeter than a dill pickle. Maybe it's a big candy stick."

He groaned with pleasure and placed his hands at the back of her head and pressed them tighter. "That sounds better."

Longarm stood there for about five minutes floating in a sea of passion and pleasure. Then he pulled back and slowly began to undress Sally Mercado. "You have the most beautiful skin. It's golden."

"I'm glad you like it."

He finished undressing her and clucked his tongue in admiration. "Sally, you are more beautiful than I remembered."

"And I remember what you do next," she said, easing back on the bed.

Longarm knelt and she raised her legs. He gently licked her juicy treasure and rested her legs on his shoulders as she sighed, then moaned and began to undulate with her hips.

"That is so good, Custis! So very good. Don't stop!"

He had no intention of stopping. Longarm plunged his face into her wetness and rooted and ravaged until Sally Mercado went wild. Then he pulled back, wiped her juices from his face, and turned her over so that she was half on and half off the bed.

"Take me!" she begged. "Take me now!"

Longarm jammed his throbbing tool up between her legs and into her honey pot, then began to pump her slowly but forcefully. Around and around until her fists were clenched and she was begging for it all, facedown into the soft bed cover.

"You want it all, here it comes!" he cried in a hoarse voice as he began to slam his slick rod in and out faster and faster until he was out of his mind and spewing his seed into her twitching body.

Sally screamed, beat the bed with joy, and shook her long black hair before she collapsed facedown. Then, she twisted around and pushed her butt up higher on him and said, "Enough of me for now?"

"Enough," Longarm panted. "Plenty enough for right now."

"Me, too," she said, her bottom still thrust upward onto his shaft.

Longarm retracted his manhood and then tenderly kissed both of her sweet buttocks. "You're worth everything a man could give," he said. "And then some."

She smiled and rolled over onto her back. "And you, Custis, are a man to remember."

He lay down beside her and stared up at the white canopy, feeling empty but completely satisfied. "So do I have to go back to my room tonight?"

"I might shoot you if you tried."

"Then I'll stay here," he said, grinning. "Do you have any more wine?"

"Some brandy. I have some excellent brandy and whiskey."

"Maybe I'll have a little of both."

She laughed. "You're a glutton."

He leaned over and kissed her huge golden breasts.

137

"Yes, I am. And before the night is over, I'll prove it to you."

"I can hardly wait."

After that, they sipped brandy and whiskey and Longarm finally got around to asking the questions that had brought him all the way to Arizona. "Now that we're alone and no one can overhear us, tell me what you really think happened to Benton, Corwin, and Tucker. I can understand how someone with ambitions to high political office would assassinate Governor Benton. Political assassinations have been taking place for centuries. But local marshal Corwin and federal marshal Ben Tucker were smart, tough law officers. To trap and kill that pair would have required someone with real skill and daring. Who could have done it?"

"There is a man in Skull Valley," she said slowly. "He owns one hell of a lot of ranch land and raises purebred cattle and racing horses. He's very rich and powerful."

"What's his name?" Longarm asked.

"His name," Sally replied, "is Captain Ira Fulton."

"Is the man a Civil War veteran?"

"Fulton was a sea captain, or so he claims. The story I've heard most often about Captain Fulton is that he made his fortune hauling Chinese whores to San Francisco during the height of the forty-niner gold rush and then selling them to the highest bidders. He also brought many of the coolies that worked on the Central Pacific Railroad in the late sixties. I have also heard that he was very big in the opium trade and still has his tentacles into that business."

"The captain sounds like a real saint," Longarm said cryptically.

"Oh, he's *anything* but a saint. Still, he's a little long in the tooth to be an assassin and he's pretty crippled with rheumatism. Despite that, I've more than once seen him take a club to much younger men and leave them bloodied and physically broken."

"Do you think Captain Fulton has political ambitions?"

Sally pursed her lips and considered the question. "I don't know Captain Fulton well . . . because I've never wanted to. I can say that he doesn't leave his ranch often and I think he does most of his buying down in Wickenburg. But sometimes he will come into Prescott with his son and they stay here at my hotel."

"How often?"

"About once a month. They are finicky about their food and drink, demanding the very best, and they expect to be waited on hand and foot. Personally, I dread seeing them walk through my doors, but they do pay very well. Captain Fulton always leaves me a fifty-dollar tip."

"What about the son?"

Sally smiled. "Oh, Frank is a fine one, he is! Quite the dandy. Pretty, like a coral snake and just as deadly with a knife or gun."

"Any chance that he might be behind the murders?"

"I don't know. Frank Fulton stands to inherit his father's fortune because he's the captain's only child—thank God. So I'm not sure why he would want to be governor of this territory. Frank's real interests are gambling and women. He calls himself a gentleman rancher and a shootist. People around here tend to get out of his way. He has no friends, only enemies."

"I'll bet *you* don't run from him," Longarm said.

"No. Frank understands that I'd kill him in his sleep, if he knocked me around or insulted me like he does most men and women. So we have a good . . . good understanding." Sally shrugged her bare shoulders and laughed. "Besides, Frank admires my style."

"That's probably not all he admires," Longarm dead-panned.

She looked at him closely. "Why, Custis, are you *jealous*?"

Longarm shook his head. "Not really."

She made a pout. "Then I'm hurt."

"I don't believe that for a minute, Sally. But Captain Fulton and his son sound like they might be the kind of men who would be behind the assassination of Arizona's next territorial governor."

"That makes sense, but why would they have anything to do with the disappearance of either Marshal Corwin or Marshal Tucker?"

"I can't answer that," Longarm replied. "And the Fulton men might be completely innocent. But I don't have any other possible suspects. There were no witnesses to the murders of Benton or Corwin and my friend Ben Tucker has just disappeared."

Sally lit a cigarette and handed it to Longarm, who declined. She said, "Are you going to Skull Valley to see Captain Ira Fulton?"

"Unless I turn up something better to do by morning." He yawned. "Do you think I'd be wasting my time?"

"No," Sally replied, "I don't. Because while Captain Fulton is the kind of man who might not want to be in the eye of the public, I have no doubt that he'd want to pull the strings of whoever was in political office."

"And his son, Frank?"

Sally blew a smoke ring toward the ceiling and considered her next words. "I'm quite sure that Frank always wants to be on parade. He likes attention and calling the shots."

"But he sounds like the kind of man who wouldn't get votes except at the point of a gun barrel."

"Frank can be a charmer. And he has his father's fortune.

I don't know. Maybe he isn't interested in political office. That's something we never really got around to talking about." She winked. "You know what I mean?"

"Yeah," Longarm said, "I'm afraid that I do."

"Just one thing you should know before you go to see the captain."

"What's that?"

"He's got a quick and violent temper. One much worse than even that of his son. So whatever you do, don't accuse the captain of anything unless you have some evidence to back it up. Otherwise—"

"Otherwise what?"

"You might wind up missing just like your friend Marshal Tucker."

"I'll keep that in mind," Longarm said. "Anyone else I ought to be looking at for these crimes?"

"Not that I can think of offhand," Sally answered. "But I wouldn't be surprised if Clyde Potts is a stooge for whoever you are looking for. That man would sell his mother for a silver dollar. I think Potts is hoping to get appointed local marshal by whoever calls the shots when all the dust clears."

Longarm considered that for a few moments. "So you think that Potts could tell me who pulls his strings, if I put some serious pressure on the man?"

"Yeah, because Potts is weak and selfish. I'm sure you could get some answers from him before you start for Skull Valley."

"Good advice. I threw him out of the marshal's office. Where would he go?"

"He stays at the old, run-down Rock Hotel. It's cheap and dirty like he is, and he has a woman there, or so I'm told."

"What kind of a woman would suffer a sorry excuse for a man like Clyde Potts?" Longarm asked.

"The kind you would expect. An old, worn-out whore

141

who has long since run out of time and money. Potts lets her stay in his room. I don't even want to think of what she has to do in return."

Longarm remembered Clyde Potts and the stench the man had left on the cot. "I don't suppose you know the name of this poor wretch."

"Irma. Irma is the only name she is known by. She was locked up in the Yuma Prison for five years after murdering a man. Some said the man deserved what he got because he was drunk and when he couldn't get his rod stiff, he forced a broom handle into Irma."

Even Longarm was appalled. "A wooden broom handle?"

"That's right. It must have hurt Irma real bad and when he was finished, the sonofabitch turned his back to her and started to get dressed and that's when Irma got up and shoved a long butcher knife up his ass. Not satisfied, she cut his throat from ear to ear and then cut off his cock and balls and tossed them out into the street. They said they could hear the man screaming and Irma laughing from a half mile away that night."

Longarm shook his head. "Irma sounds like the perfect age and an even match for old Captain Fulton."

"She would be, but he wouldn't have her on the worst day of his life so she settled for Clyde Potts."

"True love," Longarm said, taking the cigarette out of Sally's mouth and grinding it out as he pushed her back on the bed. "How would the world survive without it?"

Sally cackled with mirth and then she opened her legs and pulled Longarm back inside.

Chapter 18

Longarm knew where the Rock Hotel was located and he set out early the next morning to pay Clyde Potts and Irma a visit. He was a little hung over from his drinking and weak in the knees from all the wild lovemaking he'd enjoyed with Sally Mercado. That woman was insatiable and she hadn't let him off this morning until Longarm had administered one more good mattress pounding.

Longarm stopped outside the Rock Hotel and checked his pocket watch. It was a little after eight o'clock and many people had already been up for hours. But Longarm was pretty sure that Clyde Potts didn't have a real job nor did the dangerous old whore Irma. So instead of going directly into the shabby hotel, he found a small bakery across the street and sat for a quarter hour drinking strong black coffee and eating pastries. It wasn't his normal breakfast, but after last night's revelry, Longarm's stomach was running riot and grumbling with unhappiness. The truth of it was that he had the runs and had already raced to the outhouse several times since leaving Sally.

Ah, he thought, *the wages of excessive dissipation only got worse as a man aged.*

"One more refill of your excellent coffee," Longarm said, tipping the owner of the bakery. "And then I'm on my way."

The bakery owner was a cheerful man with red cheeks and a ready smile. "Fine morning it is. Gonna be warm and sunny today. Probably all week. You new to Prescott?"

"Yep. Just stopping in for a while."

"Business, huh?"

"You could say that," Longarm replied, not wanting to elaborate. From his counter seat he could see the Rock Hotel and no one had entered or departed that sorry structure since he'd been watching.

"Have a good day," Longarm said, slurping down the dregs of his refill and feeling his guts cramp. "You got a shitter out back?"

"Yep. Hope my pastry or strong coffee didn't give you indigestion."

"Nope. I had the runs before I got here." Without further explanation, Longarm rushed out the back and did his urgent business.

When he returned five minutes later, the baker reached down behind a shelf and gave Longarm a medicinal powder. "Drink it with another swallow of coffee," he said, pouring a bit more into Longarm's cup. "It'll settle the bowels and leave you feeling a whole lot more chipper."

"You sure?"

"Of course I am. I have a very delicate stomach and this powder soothes my bowels just like silk soothes the skin of a beautiful woman."

Longarm swallowed the powder along with a gulp of coffee and headed out the door. "Thanks."

"Good luck with your business. Stop by again soon!"

Longarm headed across the street and entered the cracked and peeling Rock Hotel. Twenty years ago, it had probably been new and even impressive, but no longer.

He'd seen hundreds of frontier hotels that had fallen into this sorry state and they all had the same disgusting smell, a mixture of piss and vomit very much like low-class saloons. A plank spanning a pair of oak barrels served as a registration desk, but there was no one in sight. Longarm leaned on the plank and noticed that there were three filthy chairs in the lobby that even an outcast Paiute Indian wouldn't have touched.

Longarm waited a minute for someone to appear and help him at the desk. Then he gave up and shouted. "Hey! I need some help here!"

He heard a thump, and then a toothless codger staggered out of a back room. He wiped his face and reeked of cheap liquor. "You need a room?"

"I need to find Clyde Potts and Irma."

The man wiped his mouth again and squinted his watery red eyes at Longarm. "What for?"

Longarm briefly considered grabbing the man by the front of his shirt and shaking him like a rat, but he decided the poor derelict already had enough grief on his plate so he gave the man four bits and said, "That's my business and none of your own."

"Right," the drunk said, pointing. "Go down that hall, three doors on the right."

"The room got a number on the door?"

"Nope." He pocketed the change and chuckled. "But I don't reckon even a fucking blind man could get lost in that narrow old hallway."

"You got a point there," Longarm answered, seeing the humor of it. "Are Clyde and Irma in their room?"

"In. Out. Who cares? But yeah, they're asleep. They don't either one of them do shit for work so they might as well sleep, snore, and slobber."

Longarm turned and walked down the hallway. At the

third door, he tried the knob, found it locked, and then he reared back on one leg and kicked the door open, splintering wood.

"Hey!" Potts cried, sitting up in bed and staring as if he'd seen a ghost. "What the hell!"

Irma was a little slower on the uptake and she finally propped herself up on an elbow and asked, "What in the hell do you want, you big bastard?"

Longarm kicked the door closed behind him. He'd knocked one hinge completely off the jamb so the door hung crooked, but he didn't really care.

"You . . . You're that damned federal marshal!" Clyde Potts finally stammered. "By gawd, you're gonna have to pay for our busted door!"

"Shut up and listen," Longarm growled and found a wooden chair, which he dragged over near the bed. He straddled it backward and draped his arms across the backrest. "Potts, you've got some explaining to do."

Potts pushed himself up in the bed, bare-chested. Irma ground knuckles into her eyes and wiped some reddish-gray hair out of her lumpy face. Then she also sat up bare-chested. Neither of them was a pretty sight and it was a toss-up which one of them had the biggest, sagging tits.

Longarm leaned a little forward in the wooden chair, his right hand near the butt of his six-gun. "Tell me about Ira and Frank Fulton."

"Don't tell him jack-shit!" Irma spat. "Who the hell do you think you are, mister! You can't just bust down our door and start asking a bunch of dumb-ass questions."

"They're not dumb-ass to me," Longarm growled. "I want to know why Frank or Captain Ira Fulton wanted Governor-Elect Benton murdered. I want to know which one of them pulled the trigger on Benton, Corwin, and my friend, Deputy U.S. Marshal Ben Tucker."

"How the hell should Clyde know anything?" Irma squealed. "Get out of here!"

Longarm quickly realized that the old whore was the one calling the shots and in charge. Potts, cowardly and weak, would do exactly what she told him to do or say. That was going to make this interrogation harder because Longarm had no qualms about beating the piss out of Potts, but he wouldn't do that with a woman—even a vicious whore like Irma.

"Well, Irma, I guess you're in this as deep as Potts, huh?" Longarm said, starting to change the direction of his questioning. "I'm sure that Clyde wouldn't fart unless you told him when and how loud."

"Shut up, you big sonofabitch!" she hissed. "You may carry a marshal's badge, but here in Prescott you're nothing. Nothing, just like that other one that came acting so high and mighty."

"That would be my friend Ben Tucker," Longarm said, his voice taking on a hard edge. "So where is he now?"

Irma's eyes were filled with hate and bloodshot from drinking too much cheap liquor. She looked like she wanted to spit at Longarm and that made him lean back on the chair.

Longarm knew that this one was going to be tough because Irma wasn't afraid of much—life had already given her all its hardest knocks.

"I hear you murdered a man and spent a lot of time in the Yuma Prison," Longarm said, his voice casual. "How'd you like it?"

She blinked and the hatred was replaced by something else. "It . . . It was hell on earth. Why do you ask?"

"I'm thinking that you and Potts will both be visiting the Yuma Prison before long. But you won't get to sleep together."

Irma's hatred toward Longarm was instantly replaced

147

by her sudden fear of returning to the Yuma Prison. Long-arm saw it in her eyes and knew that the threat of prison for this old whore was far worse even than death.

Potts swallowed hard and said, "Marshal, we didn't do anything to those three people you mentioned. So there's no need to try and scare us with the talk of being sent to Yuma."

"Oh, it's more than scare talk I'm giving you," Longarm promised. "Because I can dig up proof that you were both behind the death of Governor-Elect Benton."

"The hell you say!" Irma screamed. "It wasn't us that shot him! I can't shoot worth a damn and neither can Clyde."

"Is that right, Clyde?"

"That's right," he admitted. "I'm a terrible shot."

Longarm nodded. "And Irma here, she specializes in butcher knives." Longarm patted his crotch. "Just thinking about how you cut off a man's privates makes me nervous."

"You *ought* to be nervous, the way you're threatening us!"

"I'm going to find out who's killing people around here. One way or another, I'll not leave until I have the killers under arrest. And do you know what?"

They stared and Potts finally wagged his chin. "No."

"If I can't pin the murders on Ira or Frank Fulton, then I'll pin them on the two of *you.*"

"You *are* an unholy bastard!" Irma hissed.

"Bastard enough to send you to the Yuma Prison for a second time." Longarm grinned coldly. "Potts? Has Irma here told you all about the prison down there? About how prisoners often die of the heat, literally cooking in dirt caves like animals? Or how they commit suicide—if they don't go crazy in the heat?"

Potts managed to nod. "She's talked about it some."

"I'll bet she's talked about it more than some," Longarm countered. "Irma, you were quite a bit younger when you went there. You're older and weaker now. Do you think that you can still survive Yuma?"

He had scared her nearly witless and she had trouble stammering, "I ain't goin' back for something that I didn't do. You'd have to kill me first."

"Well, that can be arranged," Longarm said, bluffing. "But it doesn't have to be that way . . . if you tell me how and why the Fultons killed Benton and two marshals."

The pair exchanged glances and Longarm knew that he needed to bait the hook just a little bit more. "You know," he added, "if you help me get evidence to arrest the Fultons for murder, there will probably be a cash reward."

"A reward?" Irma asked, suddenly alert to happy possibilities.

"That's right."

"How much?"

Longarm shrugged. "Maybe a hundred dollars."

"Shit!" Irma exploded with contempt. "That ain't nothin' for the chances we'd be taking by telling you things about the Fultons."

"How about a hundred dollars each and a pair of one-way tickets to Reno instead of the Yuma Prison? That sound good enough?"

"How do we know we'd get what you just promised?" Potts demanded.

Longarm had anticipated the question. "I'll get the money, all right. But first you have to tell me who did those murders and how."

"A hundred now," Irma bargained. "A hundred right before you go to Skull Valley to make the arrests."

Longarm considered the proposition. He now knew that this pair held the answers he desperately needed to all the important questions. And two hundred dollars plus a couple of one-way coach fares to Reno was chicken feed considering they were the keys to helping him crack the case of three murders.

"All right," he agreed. "You tell me what you know and I'll wire Denver for the cash."

"Wire them first, *then* we'll talk," Irma said, folding her arms under her sagging tits and jutting out her jaw.

Longarm figured he could take Potts off someplace and probably beat the information out of him with little effort or blood spilled. On the other hand, Longarm knew that, if he had two collaborating accounts of the murders, it would hold up better in court.

"All right," he said. "I'll get the money this morning and pay you half up front. If what you tell me rings true, then I'll pay you the rest."

"And the tickets to Reno," Irma reminded him. "Because we're going to need to get out of this town fast if anyone ever even suspects that we spilled our guts."

"A deal," Longarm said, not bothering to shake hands. "But why don't I take Potts along to the telegraph office just in case you two lose your tongues and decide to skip town on the sly."

"Where the hell would we go to?" Irma demanded, throwing up her flabby arms. "We ain't got any money to buy stagecoach or train tickets. And we're too sick and tired to go on the run."

Longarm studied the pair and concluded that Irma was right—this pair didn't have the money or the heart to go on the run. And they knew they'd never get far anyway. Also, they were both deathly afraid of being sent to the Yuma Prison. Even more afraid of that punishment than of Captain Fulton and his son, Frank.

"All right," he said. "I'll get the cash and I should be back before noon. Be dressed and ready to tell me everything. If you hold back . . ."

Longarm left the threat hanging.

Irma said, "If we held back, you couldn't send us to prison. Not without evidence we did those killings, which we did not."

Longarm got up from the chair and winked. "You know something, Irma? I believe I could come up with some creative evidence that would send you and Clyde to Yuma for the rest of your worthless lives. Are you willing to bet that I can't be that creative?"

"Bastard!" she hissed.

"Oh," Longarm said. "I'll need your testimony in writing. Do you have writing materials here? Can either one of you write and sign your name?"

"Sure," Irma said, looking offended. "We can both read and write, you arrogant bastard."

"Then I suggest you save me some time and start writing now. In fact, I'll expect you to have written down everything on how the murders were committed by the Fultons and why."

"Fuck you!" Irma cried.

"Not even in your best days," Longarm told her as he lifted the broken door and headed down the dirty and narrow hallway. He would telegraph Billy and get the cash, then return to this piss-hole hotel. And he was sure that when he did, Irma and Clyde would sing like a couple of caged canaries.

Chapter 19

"All right," Longarm said to the telegraph operator, "this time I'll make you and your company a little more money."

The man looked up and smiled. "Another telegram to Denver?"

"Yep."

Longarm unfolded the message that he'd carefully composed. It had to say enough to get Billy Vail to bite on sending three hundred dollars to pay Irma and Potts, plus their one-way train tickets and a little extra for Longarm's mounting expenses. Those expenses would soon include renting the horse and outfit that he'd need to travel over to Skull Valley.

On the other hand, Longarm knew that if he said too much, the telegraph operator would know of his plans and the man just might blab to some of the people in town. For these reasons, the telegraph he was sending had to say just enough, but not too much.

"Here goes," Longarm said. "Are you ready?"

The man poised his finger over the key. "Go ahead, Marshal."

Billy. Need $300 to get necessary proof and information. Full explanation later. Have finally gotten what we need to make arrest. Expect to have all answers in less than three days. Wire money immediately. Custis

"That's it," Longarm said, when the man had finished tapping out the message. He sure hoped that Billy would wire the money within the hour. "What's it cost me this time?"

"Just one dollar and seventy-five cents," the operator said, not able to hide his disappointment. "Not much considering you're requesting three hundred dollars of my government's money."

"Here," Longarm replied, handing the man two silver dollars. "Keep the change."

The telegraph operator nodded his thanks. Longarm said, "I'll be in the restaurant waiting for the money. When it arrives, send word."

"Cost you fifty cents extra for a messenger boy."

Longarm gave the man his money with a stern warning. "Just don't sit on that three hundred for an extra hour or two, or I'm going to be damned upset with you, mister."

"I won't," the operator promised. "Provided you get the money you're asking for."

"I'll get it," Longarm said with more confidence than he felt.

Billy Vail was notoriously tight with his budget and three hundred dollars was the most that Longarm had ever requested without a detailed explanation. Still, Billy would know that solving the murder of Benton, the next territorial governor of Arizona, was going to be a huge feather in his cap, possibly even leading to a promotion for them both. Added to that incentive was the deaths of Marshal Corwin and their mutual friend Marshal Ben Tucker, so the stakes

154

were very high. High enough by far to induce Billy to send the money on good faith alone.

Longarm left the telegraph office and crossed the lobby to the restaurant to wait anxiously until Billy wired the money. He didn't see Sally in the main dining room so he went upstairs to her room and knocked on the door.

"What's taken you so long?" she asked, still dressed in a negligee but putting on her powder and makeup. "I've missed you!"

She kissed Longarm and fondled his privates, but he pulled back and held her at arm's length. "Sally," he said, "I'd like to make love with you again, but I'm just not up for it right now."

"I'll bet I can change your mind."

"Look," he said, "I'm expecting my boss to wire me three hundred dollars within the next hour and now I'll tell you why I need the money."

When Longarm was finished telling Sally about his arrangement with Irma and Clyde Potts, she said, "Can you trust that sleazy pair?"

"Yeah, because Irma turned about three shades of white when I told her I'd find a creative way to dig up enough evidence to send her back to the Yuma Prison. She's obviously told Potts all about that prison hellhole and he wants no part of it, either. So after that threat and the promise of two hundred cash plus a pair of train tickets to Reno, they're willing to write down in detail what happened to Benton, Corwin, and my friend Tucker. They as much as told me that Ira Fulton and his son, Frank, are behind all those murders."

"But why?"

"I don't know yet," Longarm said honestly. "I expect, when I hand Irma and Potts the money and they provide their written statements, then I'll have the answer to your question."

"What if they just lie for the money and the chance to leave town?"

Longarm shook his head. "Believe me, Sally, they won't. They know I'd track them down. Probably catch them at the train station or waiting for a stagecoach. Then they know I'd fabricate some information to tie them to the murders and send them down to Yuma."

"You'd actually do that?"

"Not really. But you're the only one I'd admit that to."

"Good," she said. "I detest Potts, but I kind of admire old Irma for what she did to the man that raped her with a broom handle. To my way of thinking, she should never have gone to prison. But it was an all-male jury and I guess the idea of a woman castrating and cutting a man's cock off was just too shocking for them to let justice be done and set Irma free."

"I guess," Longarm said, flopping in a seat. "Who in this town can you recommend to rent a horse, saddle, and gear?"

"Go down the street to the Hooker Livery. Tell Abe Hooker Jr. that I sent you and expect you to be treated the same way he's treated here at my hotel."

Longarm stared. "Do you—"

"Do I screw young Abe?"

"Yeah."

She laughed and placed a hand on her cocked hip. "Only on his birthday, which he tries to convince me comes around about six times a year."

Longarm realized the coffee was wearing off and he yawned. "Sally, are you gonna be here awhile?"

"I'm going downstairs to check on things, but I'll be back soon."

"Think I'll lie down and take a quick nap."

"Suit yourself. What's the matter? Did I wear you out last night?"

"Fact is that you did, but I recover fast."

"I hope so," she said, dressing. "So you're off to Skull Valley all alone?"

"That's the way it usually works."

"You're going to run into a beehive when you get to the captain's ranch. He has men and they will try to protect him, even from a federal marshal."

"I'm expecting that," Longarm admitted. "I'll just have to get the drop on Ira and Frank."

Sally looked worried. "Custis, how would you like a couple of good men to help? Men who won't run if bullets fly and who can shoot straight and stand tall."

"I'd like that fine. But I really can't pay or deputize them."

"I'll pay them," Sally told him. "I'll pay them well. In addition, the men that I'm thinking about hate both the Fultons."

"Why?"

"They've been cheated and bullied by both the father and son. In one case, a ranch was taken over illegally by the captain. In another case, the man was ambushed and nearly died. But he knows that the bullet came by orders of the captain. I could go on and tell you the reasons of the others, but you get the picture."

Longarm nodded. "I just don't want to take a bunch of hotheads over to Skull Valley and start a war. These men you're thinking of have to understand that they only shoot *after* I shoot. This is not a personal vendetta, Sally. I mean to arrest the captain and his son for three important and cold-blooded murders. I want them to stand trial and hang, not be gunned down by a mob of vengeance seekers."

157

"I'll make that very plain," she said. "Should five do it?"

"Five good, brave men will be plenty." Longarm smiled with relief. "Sally, I can't thank you enough. I have to admit that I was worried about how I was going to ride up to the Fulton ranch house and just arrest them for triple murders. From what I've heard, they won't come without a fight."

"You'd best believe that they won't," Sally predicted. "Unless you and the five I send get the drop on them and they have no choice except to surrender."

Longarm removed his boots and went over to the bed. "I'm tired and that whiskey and brandy we drank last night gave me the scoots. The baker down the street gave me some medicine for my upset bowels, but I'm still feeling a little rocky."

"Then take your nap. As soon as I've done a few things downstairs and then rounded up the five men that I have in mind, we'll be back."

Longarm yawned again. "Thanks, Sally."

"You can thank me in my bed when this is over as only you know how."

"I'll do that," he said, closing his eyes. "But next time, let's eat more and stick to drinking beer."

"Fine with me so long as we do it all night," Sally called as she left her room. "Sweet dreams, Marshal!"

Longarm thought about what might happen when he got the written statements from Irma and Potts. If the statements were incomplete or unsatisfactory, he'd have the pair do a rewrite. He'd make sure he had everything he needed to make an arrest of the captain and his wild son, Frank.

After all, Irma and Potts were being paid well. Probably the biggest payday of their sorry lives. And as for the tickets to Reno, well, good riddance. Arizona's gain would soon be Nevada's loss.

Longarm was sure glad that Sally was going to find five good gunmen to back up his play. It would give him all the edge that he needed in a place called Skull Valley.

Chapter 20

When Longarm went to get his written statements from Irma and Potts, he knew the moment he entered the Rock Hotel that something was very wrong. The registration plank and book were lying on the floor and a chair was overturned.

"Anyone here!" he called, expecting the toothless old derelict he'd seen earlier to shamble out of a back room.

But there was no one around to answer.

"Hey!" Longarm called as he went back to investigate. Moments later, in a tiny room he saw the toothless man lying in a large pool of fresh blood. Longarm didn't have to bend down to see that the man had been stabbed to death.

Longarm whirled around and raced up the hallway to Irma and Potts's room. Its door had been pulled partially shut and it was easy for Longarm to imagine the grisly scene that he'd discover on the other side. He knocked the door completely off its hinges and then found the mutilated bodies of Irma and Clyde Potts.

Knowing it was a waste of time, Longarm still felt for their pulses and confirmed their deaths. He looked around shaking his head. The entire room was wrecked with tables and chairs overturned and blood splattered everywhere. He hurried over to an open window and gazed up and down an empty alley. The killer—or killers—had made a clean escape and Longarm figured it had probably been within the last hour.

Longarm was so angry and frustrated that he wanted to pound his fists against the walls. Forcing himself to calm down, he carefully studied the murder scene and noted that Irma had fallen near the window and that her knuckles were scraped and her face was badly bruised. She was lying on her back with a bone-handled knife sticking out of her chest. Clyde Potts rested facedown on the bed with two deep stab wounds in his back that had probably severed his spinal cord. That told Longarm that Potts had died like a sacrificial lamb, but Irma had fought like a lion while trying to make a desperate escape through the window.

Longarm knew that these people were dead because someone had seen him enter the Rock Hotel several hours ago and had assumed he was there seeking answers and names to the killings. And the murderers knew that Irma and Potts would talk plenty and that was why they'd been brutally murdered into silence. As for the old derelict lying stabbed behind the registration desk, it was almost certain that his only sin had been to witness the murderers in the hotel's lobby.

Longarm carefully examined the room one more time and that's when he saw a few pages of bloodstained stationery lying on the floor partially hidden under the overturned kitchen table. He rushed over to the papers and when he turned them right side up, he saw at once that they were the written statements he'd told Irma and Potts to write before he returned with their money.

Longarm quickly read the statements. The one that Irma had written in her small hand was the most detailed and it

162

spelled out clearly that both Captain Ira Fulton and his son, Frank, had been involved in the murders of Governor-Elect Benton as well as the local and federal marshals. Irma's statement also said that she was sure that Captain Benton intended for his son to be the next governor of Arizona.

Potts wrote a slightly different version, but he, too, said that the Fultons were definitely behind the murders. He thought that the father and son might not have actually committed the crimes, but instead had them committed by their paid gunmen. Potts also said that he had been promised the job of Prescott town marshal by Captain Fulton as a reward for keeping his silence.

Longarm took a deep breath and said to the bodies, "Sorry you didn't make it to Reno, but thanks for these statements. I assure you that the captain and his son, Frank, will both be joining you in the local cemetery before long."

Longarm neatly folded the bloodstained papers and placed them in his vest pocket. Then he climbed out the window and moved down the alleyway looking for evidence the killers might have left on their hasty exit.

He emerged from the alley without any important clues other than the fact that he'd found a few drops of dark, sticky blood. Longarm was sure that meant that Irma had managed to wound one of the men who murdered her, but probably not badly. The wound might well have been the result of a desperate punch to the nose. Longarm made a mental note to remind himself to see if Frank Fulton had a broken nose or some other visible injury.

"I'll give you this much, Irma," Longarm said to himself. "You didn't go out with a whimper. If Potts had put up half as good a fight as you did, things might have turned out better for you both."

Longarm went back to the St. Michael Hotel and told Sally what he'd found and discovered. He removed the bloodstained written statements from his pocket and gave them to her with instructions. "If I'm killed in Skull Valley trying to arrest the captain and his son, then I want you to get these statements to my boss, Billy Vail, at the Federal Building in Denver. Take them there personally and tell him everything I've told you."

"Maybe five men aren't enough," she said, taking the statements. "Maybe I should try to find more—or you should wait for your boss to send help."

"I'm not a man who likes to wait," Longarm replied. "Where are these five men?"

"I told them to get ready to ride and meet you at the Hooker Livery. They're probably waiting there for you right now."

"Sally, I could make good use of a double-barreled shotgun."

"There's one loaded and resting behind the bar downstairs. You'll find a box of extra shells there, too. Help yourself."

He hugged and kissed her. "I'll be back in a few days."

"Remember what I said about Captain Fulton. If he suspects that you have the evidence to arrest him or his son, he'll try to kill you in a hurry."

"I'll remember." Longarm started for the door. "And don't you forget what I said about getting those letters to my boss in Denver. Irma and Potts weren't much, but their letters will put nooses around Ira and Frank Fulton's necks."

"I hope that I don't have to take them to Denver," Sally replied. "But I will if I must."

That was all that Longarm needed to hear. He didn't know how many gunmen were waiting for him in Skull Valley, but even if he and five good men died, he wanted the Fultons to pay for all the murdering that had taken place right here in Prescott.

Chapter 21

The five men that Sally Mercado had promised to help Longarm turned out to be only three. Longarm didn't ask why the other two had changed their minds about riding to Skull Valley, because it didn't matter. The three who had shown up armed to the teeth looked like tough, determined men. Whether or not they were good with their guns and would make a stand if bullets began to fly was yet to be seen.

The Penny brothers had lost their ranch to Captain Ira Fulton because he'd dammed and then diverted their only water supply, a tributary of the Verde River. Bill Penny, the oldest brother, couldn't hide his bitterness when he said, "Our parents homesteaded our ranch land and for years everyone shared the Verde River water. Then Captain Fulton moved in upriver and cut off the river. He might as well have cut our throats. Without water we lost everything, and the captain wound up getting our family's homestead for pennies on the dollar at an auction sale."

"Sorry about that," Longarm told the brothers. "But you have to understand that we're not riding to Skull Valley with the sole purpose of killing Captain Fulton or Frank so you can get your revenge."

"Then what the hell are we goin' there for?" Jesse Penny, the younger brother demanded.

Longarm looked right into their angry eyes. "We're going there to arrest the captain and Frank for the murder of Governor-Elect Benton and two law officers, one of them a friend of mine out of the Denver Federal Building."

The brothers were clearly disappointed, but if all they wanted to do was kill the Fultons, then he was better off without their help.

"And what about you?" he asked the third man who was homely but tough-looking and powerfully built. He looked like a farmer, but he might have been a cattleman. "What's your grudge against the Fultons?"

"I'd rather not talk about why I hate Frank Fulton," the man said, square jaw clenching.

"Well," Longarm said, trying to measure this man, "I sure don't want to pry into your business or life, but I have to know why you've volunteered for what could be a bad gunfight."

He jammed his thumbs into his gun belt and his eyes narrowed. "You mean I have to tell you my reasons or you won't let me ride along to this fight?"

"That's about the size of it," Longarm replied.

The man stood beside his roan horse and struggled with his next words. "Okay, damnit. My name is Odie Dunbar and I have a little ranch southwest of town. It ain't big, but I'm doin' pretty good and I work real hard."

"I'm sure that you do," Longarm said. "So why do you want to ride into a gunfight against long odds of winning?"

"Well, Marshal, if you must know, I was engaged to marry Miss Claire McClure. But then Frank Fulton came along and told her lies and . . . Well . . . he did her wrong, then left her and bragged about it to everyone in Prescott."

Odie's voice grew hoarse with emotion and he looked

166

away quickly, but didn't stop talking. "My Claire couldn't live with her shame and killed herself last Wednesday. I was the only one that was at her burial. Not even her parents would come to—"

Odie's voice broke and his eyes filled with tears. Longarm's heart went out to Odie, but he still had to make sure there would be no mistakes when they reached Skull Valley.

Softening his voice, Longarm said, "Odie, I've heard enough to know that Frank Fulton considers himself quite a ladies' man and I know that he has both good looks and his father's money. But I also know that he can't be much of a real man."

Odie swallowed hard and then hissed, "I mean to see him *dead* for what he did to my sweetheart! I'm gonna kill him or he's gonna kill me. There's no other way around it."

They were standing beside their horses at the stable and townspeople were watching from a distance. Longarm glanced over at the Penny brothers who looked damned uncomfortable, so he said, "Bill. Jesse. Would you boys mind taking your horses over there a distance so Odie and I can have a word or two in private?"

"Sure," Bill Penny said, leading his horse off followed by his brother.

Longarm chose his next words carefully. "Odie, here's the thing about this deal. I have proof that the captain and his son, Frank, murdered or had murdered Benton, Corwin, and Tucker. Now I mean to arrest the Fultons and see them hang. I'm a sworn officer of the law, not a hired gunman, and I have to at least try to arrest the Fultons and see that they get a trial."

"Marshal, what you don't seem to understand is that the Fultons will hire expensive lawyers and get off scot-free," Odie said, bitterly. "And Frank will never go to jail for what he did to my fiancée. He killed her just the same as he did them three you just mentioned."

"I'm sure that's true," Longarm said, "and I'm sorry about your fiancée . . . but I can't take you along if you are hell-bent on shooting Frank down on sight. And the other thing is that I really could use you today. Are you good with a gun?"

"Not as good as Frank Fulton, but I'll be a hell of a lot tougher to kill."

"I'd like you to come with us, Odie. But I have to have your word you won't pull your gun unless I do first. You have to promise me that you'll let me try to arrest them for murder."

Odie toed the earth and he was obviously caught in a hard dilemma. Odie was a powerful-looking young man, but certainly not handsome. It was plain to see how a good-looking and rich rival like Frank Fulton could have turned poor Miss McClure's head with well-practiced sweet talk and empty promises. To Frank Fulton, Miss McClure would have just been another sexual conquest, but to Odie, Miss McClure had probably been the promise of his lifetime.

"Odie?" Longarm finally asked. "What's your answer?"

He looked up and said, "Them Fultons won't surrender to you, Marshal. They'll try to gun you and the Penny brothers down."

"In that case, we'll be fighting for our lives," Longarm said. "All four of us against however many are at that ranch."

Odie said, "We'll be outnumbered at least two to one."

"All the more reason why I want you to come along."

"Okay," Odie said, sticking out his calloused hand to shake on their deal. "I won't do or say anything until you go for your gun. Then I'll be right behind and the first man I'll shoot is Frank."

"Fair enough," Longarm agreed.

"Let's mount up!" Longarm said, jamming the shotgun into a rifle boot and then his foot into the stirrup.

So they rode out of Prescott headed for Skull Valley and what Longarm was sure would be a bloody shoot-out. He knew his own capabilities, but he hadn't a clue as to how well the Penny brothers or Odie Dunbar were going to be in a shoot-out.

It didn't matter. He'd find that out soon enough.

Chapter 22

After a long day in the saddle and the hard crossing over a range of mountains, they camped that night not more than two miles north of Captain Fulton's huge cattle ranch. All that day Longarm had been observing and trying to size up his three companions, but hadn't come to any real conclusions. The Penny brothers were cowboys, that much was plain. They were excellent horsemen and knew this country well. They were the ones who had picked a fine campsite among some large boulders where there was good water and plenty of grass for their tired horses. Both of the brothers wore six-guns and had Winchester rifles, but Longarm didn't get the sense that they were real fighters.

The Penny brothers were nervous, but determined to settle a score with Captain Fulton, and even though they'd already lost their homestead, Longarm had the impression that they had plans to make claim on the Fulton ranch for damages and new land if the captain was killed or hanged.

Odie Dunbar was much harder to read. He seemed to be by nature a shy man, quiet and unpretentious. He was physically powerful and Longarm got the impression that Odie had been in quite a few scrapes. Maybe just fistfights, but Longarm thought perhaps more. Odie carried himself and his gun as if they were part of his thick body. Instead of a Winchester, he used a big buffalo rifle that looked as if it could probably drop a man half a mile away. That rifle alone told Longarm that Odie was a marksman and a hunter. Longarm felt that Odie was dangerous like a vial of nitroglycerin and ready to explode at the slightest provocation or excuse. And who could blame him? His sweetheart had been used and discarded by Frank Fulton, then had taken her own life.

If ever a man had a reason to kill another man, it was Odie Dunbar.

The Penny brothers talked quietly that night and Longarm knew that each pledged to the other that they would stand or fall together. And if only one survived, the other would see that his sibling was buried in a special place and manner.

Odie never talked at all. He simply lay on his blankets and stared at the cold canopy of stars. Longarm thought that Odie was almost hoping to join Claire McClure because he just didn't give a tinker's damn if he lived or died.

They awoke almost two hours before dawn when dew was heaviest on the meadow grass. Without eating or starting a fire for coffee, they saddled their horses and started toward the ranch in the faint moonlight. It was Longarm's intention to ride straight up to the ranch house and then dismount and barge through the front door. If the captain and his son were sound asleep in their beds, so much the easier for his arrest.

"There it is," Odie said, pointing. "And still not a light on in either the main house or the bunkhouse. But they'll be up and about within the hour. How do you want to handle this, Marshal?"

172

"Does anyone know if they have ranch dogs?" Longarm asked.

"They do," Bill Penny said. "A big pack of 'em."

"Do they know you?"

Penny shrugged. "They used to . . . before we lost our place. I doubt that those dogs remember us anymore."

Longarm considered the possibility of sending the Penny brothers up to the house to try to silence and calm the dogs, but discarded that idea. The dogs would probably start barking as soon as they were all within a quarter mile of the house.

"What's behind the house?" Longarm asked, squinting at the distant dark shadows.

Bill said, "A barn and corrals. Can I make a suggestion, Marshal?"

"Sure."

"Why don't you send me and my brother around behind the barn. We can come into the main house from the back door off the kitchen. We both know the layout of the house. Meanwhile, you and Odie can just gallop through the yard and go through the front door."

"Where is the bunkhouse?" Longarm asked.

Bill Penny pointed. "It's that dark shape off to the right of the house."

"How many men stay there?"

"Maybe ten or a dozen."

"Does it only have one front door?"

Penny thought a minute. "Yeah. But—"

Longarm cut him off. "I want you and your brother to ride for the bunkhouse. Try to block the door and keep the hands inside while Odie and I go into the house for the captain and Frank."

"How are we going to keep a dozen men inside that bunkhouse?" Jesse Penny asked.

"You'll figure out something," Longarm told the younger brother. "If you can keep the hands corralled, Odie and I shouldn't have a problem."

The brothers exchanged glances and the older one said, "We'd rather go for the main house. Why don't *you* take care of the bunkhouse, Marshal?"

Longarm knew the Penny brothers wanted to gun down the captain and Frank without any hesitation, so he said, "Because I'm the one that's arresting the Fultons and making the decisions here. You boys got a problem with that?"

The brothers weren't happy, but they shook their heads and checked their guns one last time.

"Then let's go," Longarm said, tightening his cinch. "We'll ride straight for the house and bunkhouse and when the dogs start barking, we make a charge. Ready, Odie?"

"More than ready," he said.

"Good. Let's ride and no talk. When the dogs bark, we charge."

And that was just the way it happened. Longarm and his three companions got within about two hundred yards of the buildings before the first dog let out a sleepy bark. They spurred their horses into a run and minutes later were into the yard and scattering the pack of Fulton dogs.

Longarm and Odie dived off their horses and charged up the big veranda, then through the front door. It was dark inside and Longarm spilled over a box of apples and crashed headlong into the hallway. He heard curses and shouts and then a light went on in a room down the hallway.

"What the hell is going on out there!" A moment later, a big, barefooted old man in a nightshirt appeared with a lantern.

"Marshal Custis Long. You're under arrest, Captain!"

The old man jumped back into his bedroom and locked his door before Longarm could get off a shot.

Odie yelled, "I'm going to look for Frank!"

"Don't gun him down!" He turned back toward the bedroom door. "Open up, Captain!"

Longarm heard the cock of a gun's hammer and a moment later three bullets splintered through the locked door. "You're a dead man, Marshal!"

Longarm heard gunfire in another part of the house. Half a dozen shots or more. "Odie!"

No answer. Longarm charged the captain's door, slamming into it with his left shoulder, but it was far heavier and better made than the one in the Rock Hotel and didn't budge. He shot the doorknob twice before he tried to barge through a second time.

But the locks still held. "Captain, you better open up or a lot of men are going to die, including your son!"

"Go to hell!"

Longarm couldn't get through the door and maybe it was best that he did not. If the captain was waiting on the other side with a gun, the old seaman would have a huge killing advantage.

Longarm turned and ran down the hallway, not sure where he was going next. He slammed into Odie and they both crashed to the floor amid a bunch of apples that were rolling around.

"What the— Marshal!"

"Where's Frank!" Longarm yelled, scrambling to his feet and kicking apples in all directions.

"Frank escaped through the front door."

Longarm sprinted through the living room and outside. The light was now sufficient enough to see that the Penny brothers were pinned down behind a wagon and that Fulton men—most in nighshirts—had managed to escape the bunkhouse and were returning a withering fire.

"What do we do!" Odie cried.

"We'd better jump into that fight or Bill and Jesse are finished," Longarm said, grabbing the borrowed shotgun from his saddle and then taking cover. Odie ran to his horse, grabbed the buffalo rifle, and joined him.

"I take it you know how to use that big sonofabitch pretty well," Longarm said.

"You take it right," Odie replied, cocking the rifle and taking quick aim.

"Then put some fear in them," Longarm ordered.

And Odie did just that. His buffalo rifle repeatedly thundered with the ferocity of a small cannon, sending panicked cowhands scrambling for cover back into the bunkhouse. Longarm saw three men go down who would never again get to their feet and still Odie kept firing as methodically as a machine. His rifle was so powerful it was blowing slugs right through the bunkhouse walls.

"Keep it up," Longarm commanded. "No one is coming out of there now."

Longarm turned and ran around the house. He just caught a glimpse of a nightshirt disappearing around the barn and he knew the captain was waiting in ambush.

Longarm took cover in the hay barn. It was pitch-dark so he backed out with the shotgun, then began to edge along the walls. In the east, a faint line of gray was beginning to appear. It would be daylight in less than fifteen minutes, but Longarm figured that this bloody business would soon be over—one way or another.

"Captain!"

Captain Fulton was just around the corner and when he jumped out and opened fire, Longarm pulled both barrels of the shotgun and blew him down like wheat before a scythe. He hurried over to the rancher and then recoiled to see that the captain had caught both barrels in the neck and head. There wasn't enough still attached on top of the old man's shoulders to fill a poor man's tobacco pouch.

Longarm heard the sound of hoofbeats pounding across the yard and he twisted and ran back toward the house.

"You cowardly sonofabitch!" Odie screamed, jumping up from cover and charging after the horse on foot, then dropping to one knee and taking aim.

Frank Fulton was almost out of sight. Almost safe in the poor light when Odie fired from a kneeling position. Longarm saw Fulton sag on his galloping horse and slump over its neck a moment before it disappeared.

Odie started to run after Frank, but someone from the bunkhouse shot him. Odie tried to keep his legs moving, but he was shot a second time and fell hard. The Penny brothers started firing into the bunkhouse as fast as they could work their weapons.

Longarm yelled at them to keep the men pinned down inside. He then ran to his horse and mounted the skitterish animal. He sent it into a gallop after Frank Fulton.

Fulton was down less than a mile from the ranch house, but he wasn't dead. He was trying to crawl behind some rocks when Longarm saw the man and jumped off his horse. He had left his shotgun back at the house, but his six-gun was now in his hand.

"Frank, don't move," he ordered. "Drop your gun."

The sunlight was growing stronger by the moment and now Longarm could clearly see the pale, strikingly handsome face. Like his dead father, Frank was barefoot yet had had the presence of mind to put on a shirt, pants, and his gun belt.

"You're the marshal from Denver," he hissed as Longarm walked forward.

"The *second* marshal from Denver. Where's Ben Tucker?"

"Buried somewhere you'll never find!"

"Did you also kill Governor Benton and Marshal Corwin?"

"Sure!" Frank hissed. "And it was *easy*."

"Then you're under arrest for murder."

Frank cursed and a knife suddenly appeared in his right hand. The hand shot forward like a bullwhip and the throw was so hard and accurate that it was impossible for Longarm to move fast enough. The knife plunged deep into his shoulder and he felt the searing pain as he fell.

Frank went for a gun he had hidden in his belt. The gun came up and both he and Longarm fired at exactly the same instant. Longarm felt the impact of Frank's bullet and then he felt absolutely nothing.

Chapter 23

Longarm awoke several days later between Sally Mercado's silk sheets. He hurt all over, especially in the head. "Ugh," he groaned.

Sally was instantly at his side. "So you finally decided to wake up," she said, leaning over and touching the bandages. "I thought you might sleep until the Fourth of July."

"What happened?" he asked, making an effort to push himself up on his elbows and then painfully deciding that was a bad mistake.

"You're not leaving my bed anytime soon," Sally told him. "The doctor said you've lost about two bathtubs worth of blood. And that head wound was just a hair's width away from making you silly for the rest of your days."

Longarm closed his eyes. "Tell me what happened out there after I was shot by Frank."

She sat down on the bed. "The Penny brothers made the Fulton men who hadn't already been killed surrender and throw down their weapons. Then they tied them all up and came looking for you."

"What about Frank?"

"You killed him."

"I shot him after Odie had already put a big slug in him," Longarm explained. "Is Odie dead?"

"No," she said. "He ought to be, but he isn't. The doctor says that Odie Dunbar must have nine lives just like a cat. He's going to make it."

"Good," Longarm said with relief.

"I've got one of my best bar girls taking care of Odie. She says she thinks he's cute and real sweet."

"Maybe there's a chance for Odie to fall in love again," Longarm said. "At least I hope there is for his sake."

"You never know," Sally told him. "But I've some very sad news for you."

Longarm took a deep breath and winced, remembering that he'd had Frank's knife go deep into his shoulder. No wonder he hadn't been able to raise up on his arms.

"What's the sad news?"

"I took the liberty of sending a telegram to your boss. I got his address from our telegraph operator."

"And?"

"I told him all about how you got the murder evidence and had a showdown with the Fultons. I told him Captain Fulton and his son, Frank, were dead so there'd be no murder trial."

"Billy Vail probably wasn't happy about that," Longarm said.

Sally shrugged as if that was of no importance. "Your boss just said that you should come back when you were feeling up to the travel. I sent a second telegraph saying you'd be under a doctor's care here in Prescott for at least two months."

"Two months!" Longarm snorted. "Hell, I'll be headed back to Denver in a week."

"No you won't," Sally argued. "Because you and I are going to take a nice vacation up to the Grand Canyon."

"What?"

"You heard me. Custis, I know a man who has a lodge up on the south rim where we can sit all day in rocking chairs when we're not in bed making frantic love."

"Sally!"

She raised her eyebrows in question and brushed back her long black hair. "Maybe you think you need to get back to Denver and into the outstretched arms of some woman named Dilly?"

Longarm didn't know how on earth she knew about Dilly. Maybe he'd been delirious and had spoken her name a few times in this bed.

"Forget Dilly," Sally told him firmly. "Your boss telegraphed one last time to say that Dilly, or Miss Delia Hamilton—my, my doesn't she sound oh-so-upper-crust and proper! Just your type, huh?"

"Go on," Longarm grated, not appreciating the sarcasm. "What about Dilly?"

"Well, I hope this doesn't break your heart, but it seems that your Dilly fell in love with a convalescing physician named Dr. Wilson and took him to Philadelphia on the train to meet her rich parents. He asked the Hamiltons for their daughter Dilly's hand in marriage and they immediately consented."

"You have to be kidding me!"

"No, I'm afraid not. How very sad . . . but fitting." Sally leaned over and kissed Longarm on the cheek and then her hand sneaked under the silk sheets to pinch him on his privates.

"Sally!"

"Oh, don't be protesting so much," she replied with a pout. "Surely you never thought that you and some rich man's daughter from Philadelphia would ever have a chance at happiness. Why, Custis, you big sweetie, you'd have gone stark raving mad back East mired down in the straightjacket of high society."

He supposed that was the truth but it rankled him to agree, so he said, "How the hell would you know?"

"I just *know* you," Sally said. "And I know me. And I know that we'll have the best old time at the beautiful Grand Canyon."

Longarm sighed. So Dilly and the doctor had fallen in love and were engaged to be married. He realized that many things had happened in Denver since his absence, not all of them bad.

"Sally, since I'm not going back to Denver for a while there is one more thing I need to know from my boss."

"What's that?"

"Did he say he was gonna feed and take care of my tomcat, Tiger?"

Sally just stared at him and then for some strange reason, she threw back her head and began to laugh.

Watch for

**LONGARM AND THE
PINE BOX PAYOFF**

the 352nd novel in the exciting LONGARM
series from Jove

Coming in March!

GIANT-SIZED ADVENTURE FROM AVENGING ANGEL LONGARM.

BY TABOR EVANS

2006 GIANT EDITION

LONGARM AND THE OUTLAW EMPRESS
978-0-515-14235-8

2007 GIANT EDITION

LONGARM AND THE GOLDEN EAGLE SHOOT-OUT
978-0-515-14358-4

penguin.com

Jove Westerns put the "wild"
back into the Wild West.

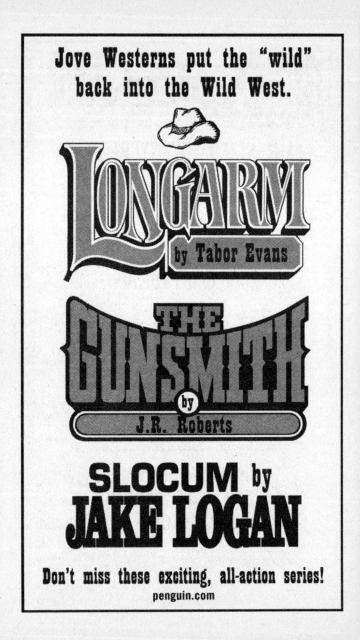

LONGARM
by Tabor Evans

THE GUNSMITH
by
J.R. Roberts

SLOCUM by
JAKE LOGAN

Don't miss these exciting, all-action series!
penguin.com

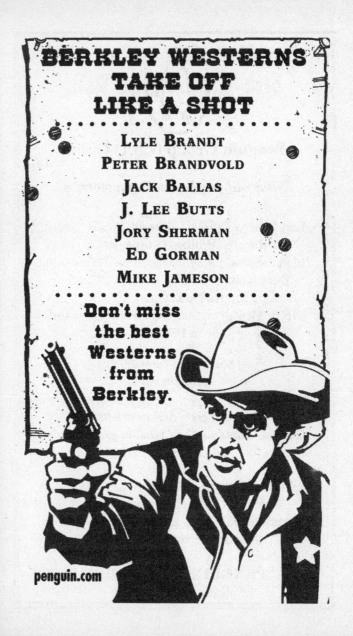

BERKLEY WESTERNS TAKE OFF LIKE A SHOT

LYLE BRANDT
PETER BRANDVOLD
JACK BALLAS
J. LEE BUTTS
JORY SHERMAN
ED GORMAN
MIKE JAMESON

Don't miss the best Westerns from Berkley.

penguin.com

Penguin Group (USA) Online

What will you be reading tomorrow?

Tom Clancy, Patricia Cornwell, W.E.B. Griffin,
Nora Roberts, William Gibson, Robin Cook,
Brian Jacques, Catherine Coulter, Stephen King,
Dean Koontz, Ken Follett, Clive Cussler,
Eric Jerome Dickey, John Sandford,
Terry McMillan, Sue Monk Kidd, Amy Tan,
John Berendt…

You'll find them all at
penguin.com

*Read excerpts and newsletters,
find tour schedules and reading group guides,
and enter contests.*

Subscribe to Penguin Group (USA) newsletters
and get an exclusive inside look
at exciting new titles and the authors you love
long before everyone else does.

PENGUIN GROUP (USA)
us.penguingroup.com